# SEALED WITH VALOR

A CHRISTIAN K-9 ROMANTIC SUSPENSE

CALLED TO PROTECT

LAURA SCOTT

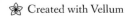

# CHAPTER ONE

Former Navy SEAL Nico Ramirez lay stretched out on a hill overlooking a dilapidated apartment building with his Doberman, Zulu, beside him. This was his first solid lead in the almost eight months he'd been trying to find his swim buddy's younger sister, Ava. Jaydon Rampart hadn't survived their last mission. The rest of their SEAL team had all suffered injuries, some worse than others. He'd been one of the more fortunate ones; he'd only been sidelined for ten weeks after having his ruptured Achilles tendon repaired. Losing Jaydon had been tough, but discovering Ava was missing had been worse. He'd felt as if he'd failed his buddy all over again.

At first, he'd thought she'd simply needed time and space to grieve her brother. He'd been healing from his own surgery too. But after one week became two, the warning bells in the back of his mind had gone off.

She was gone. Had quit her job and disappeared.

He'd followed one lead after another. He'd discovered Ava had spent time at a Los Angeles battered women's shelter back in March, but then she had vanished without telling anyone where she was going. Her boyfriend, Simon Marks, a.k.a. Simon Normandy, was the one who'd caused her to seek shelter in the first place according to Charlotte Cambridge, now Charlotte Tyson, who ran the shelter. Knowing about the abuse had made him even more determined to find her.

But every clue he'd followed up on had led to a dead end. He was beyond frustrated, yet he had refused to give up.

Would never give up. Not until he'd found her.

Finally, after what seemed like eons, Ava's friend Jill had heard from her. From what Jill had explained, Ava had been crying, saying something about needing to hear a friendly voice. Jill had tried to soothe Ava, assuring her that everything would be okay. But when Jill had pressed for details as to where she was, Ava had quickly said she had to go and disconnected from the call.

It had taken Nico several days and calling in a big favor from Bryce Flynn, one of his cop buddies who was a retired Navy SEAL turned K9 officer, to trace Ava's call. Which had led him here to San Bernardino, California.

And to this sketchy-looking apartment building.

He peered again through the binoculars. He'd been hoping to catch a glimpse of Ava going in or coming out of the building, but so far, he hadn't seen her. Or anyone who looks like her. He was certain Ava had changed her appearance in the months she'd been gone. But she couldn't change her skin color, and most of the people going in and out of the building had either been heavily tattooed white men or people of color.

The sun dipped low on the horizon as the hour headed toward seven o'clock in the evening. Mid-September meant the days were already growing short. Nico had been here for several hours, leaving only to take care of his K9 partner, Zulu, and the occasional bathroom break.

Zulu was a high-energy Doberman he'd gotten back when he and the other guys had met with Lillian, the woman who rescued dogs and helped train them for injured military vets. Mason Gray, their senior chief, had arranged for every one of them to get a dog. Lillian had been happy to accommodate them. The moment he'd set eyes on the female Doberman, Nico had known she was for him. Zulu had been an amazing partner and was extremely protective.

He watched for a few more minutes and was about to lower his binoculars to give Zulu a break when he froze. A woman crossed the street, walking toward the apartment building. She'd come from the same direction he was facing, so he could only see her from the back, but she was white with short and curly blond hair. She wore a casual yellow sundress and sandals in deference to the heat.

Ava had always worn her red hair long and straight, but that didn't mean much. He could also count on one hand how many times he'd seen her wearing a dress, she'd always lived in jeans and other casual clothes, but again, things could have changed. He slowly focused the binoculars to get a closer look at her profile.

His heart thudded against his rib cage as he watched her striding toward the door. "Come on," he whispered under his breath. "Show me your face."

As if on cue, the woman turned to glance furtively behind her as if concerned she was being followed. Nico almost dropped his binoculars when he saw Ava's familiar beautiful features etched in fear.

He'd found her! He surged to his feet. "Come, Zulu!" The apartment building wasn't secure, which he hadn't liked one bit, yet he wanted to catch Ava before she disappeared into one of the apartments. He'd already checked the names on the mailboxes, but there was no Ava Rampart.

No surprise, she'd likely changed her name to match her altered appearance.

He ran down the hill and across the street with Zulu at his side. His ruptured Achilles tendon was healed now, but it still gave him a twinge when he did things like move abruptly. Ignoring the pain, he managed to catch up to Ava just as she was crossing the threshold going inside the apartment building.

Sensing his presence, she began to run, but he urgently called, "Ava, it's me. Nico."

She spun to face him, her mouth dropping in surprise. "N-Nico? How did you find me?"

"I've been searching for you since March." Nico's gaze dropped to her belly. Her very pregnant belly. For a moment, he couldn't move, couldn't even think. The baby had to be Simon's, which only ratcheted up his anger at how the guy had physically abused her. Somehow, he managed to find his voice. "Let's go. I know you're in trouble, and I'm here to help."

She glanced furtively around, then gestured to the building. "Come inside. We can't talk here."

Zulu growled, which caused Ava to step back in fear. He put a hand on Zulu and reached out to take Ava's hand. "Friend, Zulu. Ava is a friend."

"Renee," she hissed. "I'm Renee."

"Friend, Zulu," he dutifully repeated. "Renee is a friend."

Zulu wagged her butt, her tail having been cropped before Lillian had been able to prevent it, and licked Ava's— Renee's hand. Satisfied she wasn't going to be bitten, Ava opened the door and led the way inside.

Nico remembered seeing a Renee on the mailbox for apartment number 3. Ava pulled out her key and unlocked the door, one that would buckle under a well-placed kick, he thought grimly. He kept his thoughts to himself as she gestured for him to come inside.

The place was surprisingly clean, despite the roach traps set in every corner of the small space. He swallowed hard, hating the way Ava had been forced to live like this. She closed and locked the door. Then tucked her keys back into her oversized purse that she wore crossways over her body.

In a way, that only magnified her pregnancy.

"I need to know how you found me." She walked over and sank down onto the sofa, wincing as if her feet were killing her. "Because if you found me, Simon will too."

"You've been running from him all this time?" He heard his voice rising in anger and tried to dial it back a notch. "If you would have just reached out to me, you wouldn't be stuck in a place like this. Better yet, why didn't you go to the police?"

She narrowed her eyes. "First of all, I didn't know you were looking for me. Secondly, you don't seem to understand the seriousness of the situation. I can't go to the police, there are—reasons. They don't matter right now, all that I care about is flying under the radar. Every time I think I'm safe, one of Simon's goons finds me." Her hand rested on her belly. "I need to know, Nico. How did you find me?"

"I traced your call to Jill." He came over to sit beside her. "You're not alone anymore, Ava. I'm here, and I'll keep you safe from Simon. But I need to understand why you can't go to the police."

"Jill?" Her eyes widened in horror at her mistake. She stood with a grimace. "I need to get out of here."

"I'll take care of you," he repeated. "Do you need to pack anything? Um, you know, for your baby?"

She arched a brow. "I don't have anything for the baby yet, I'm not due until the middle of November. I would like to grab some clothes, it's not easy to find maternity clothes on the run. Oh, and I need to get Callie too."

"Callie? What is that? A cat?"

Ava didn't answer, disappearing into the bedroom. He paced the small apartment, his mind whirling. Ava was having a baby by the middle of November.

Simon's baby.

No, her baby. Simon didn't deserve to have his name associated with an innocent child. Just the thought of him striking at Ava while she was pregnant made his gaze go red with fury. And what was this about not being able to go to the cops? His gut tightened. He didn't understand, but he would learn everything very soon.

But this wasn't the time or the place to grill her about Simon. If she was right about Simon and his goons finding her, they needed to get out of Dodge.

Or in this case, out of San Bernardino.

"I'm ready. And Callie isn't a cat. She's a friend." Ava stopped in the small kitchen area to grab a bottle of what looked like vitamins. She stuffed them into the backpack she held in one hand.

"I'll take that." He reached for the pack and slung it over his shoulder. "Where is Callie? Does she know Simon too?"

"Yes, we've both been trying to stay safe." Ava avoided his gaze as she headed for the door. "She'll be at work, so we'll need to pick her up on the way."

"Come, Zulu." His K9 stayed at his side as he quickly

caught up to Ava. He held his Sig Sauer pistol in his hand. "Let me go first. I want you to stay behind me."

For the first time, she seemed to soften. "Thank you, Nico."

"Always." There was so much more he wanted to say, but his questions and concerns would have to wait. Once they were in the hall, he stopped her with a hand on her arm. "Is there a back door?"

"Good point. This way." She gestured down the hall, in the opposite direction of the front door. He nodded, taking the lead with Zulu beside him.

At the back door to the building, he took a moment to rake his gaze over the area. Seeing nothing alarming, he pushed the door open and stepped out. "Stay close," he told Ava. "I left my SUV a few blocks down the road."

If he'd have known about her pregnancy, he'd have parked closer. For a nanosecond, he considered having her stay here so he could fetch the car so she wouldn't have to walk on her sore feet. But now that he'd found her, he wasn't about to let her out of his sight.

Ava didn't complain as they made their way along the back of the building. Upon reaching the corner, he paused to peer around it.

A movement caught his eye. A beefy bald guy wearing a leather vest and biker boots was lurking near the building next door. He narrowed his gaze, then turned to Ava. He put his mouth to her ear. "Is that Simon or one of his thugs?"

He moved just enough so she could see the man for herself. She stared for a long moment, then shrugged. "I don't recognize him. But that doesn't mean anything. Simon has a wide reach. He looks like he could be from Simon's gang."

Not good. Nico knew they'd need to avoid drawing the lurker's attention.

"Let's go the other way." He turned and hugged the back of the building to the other corner. It was the opposite direction from where he'd left his Jeep, but it couldn't be helped. When he reached that corner, he took another peek.

There was no one around. Breathing a sigh of relief, he led the way to the next building, and the next, until he found one where they could head around the block to where his Jeep was waiting.

Zulu was a dark shadow at his side, and he was grateful for her presence. Ava was breathing heavily by the time they arrived at his Jeep. A flash of concern hit hard. He had zero knowledge of pregnant women, but running around like this couldn't be good for her or the baby.

"Are you okay?" he asked. He holstered his weapon and opened the passenger door for her to get inside.

"I'm fine." Her curt tone didn't invite further discussion.

When she was settled, he closed the door and took Zulu around to the back hatch. The moment he opened it, Zulu jumped inside, knowing what was expected of her. Slamming it shut, he quickly went to the driver's side to get behind the wheel. "Ready? I want us to get far away from that guy lurking near your apartment building. We need to get out of the city."

"I agree, but after we pick up Callie." She struggled to get the seat belt beneath her belly. "I'm not leaving her behind to face Simon or his thugs, Nico, so don't bother arguing with me."

He ground his back molars together as he pulled away from the curb. Every instinct made him want to drive far away without looking back. But she was right, he couldn't leave another innocent woman in harm's way. "Okay, where exactly is she?"

"She's a waitress at the Lizard Lounge. It's only a few blocks from here."

He remembered passing the place on his way to the apartment building. "Do you work there too?"

"Yes." She didn't elaborate, but it explained why her feet were sore. He hated thinking about her standing and serving people all day, but he told himself to let it go. Now that he'd found her, he planned to keep her safe.

Once they were settled, he'd call the rest of his team to let them know he'd found Ava. All six members of the SEAL team had been concerned about Ava's disappearance, but as Jaydon's swim buddy, Nico had made it his personal mission to find her. His five teammates had tried to help him in various ways, despite suffering their own injuries sustained during their last op. Some of them, like Hudd, had been injured worse than others.

And weirdly, they'd all fallen in love over the past seven months. Once he'd imagined himself in love with Ava, but that had been years ago, when she'd been too young for the likes of him. Even if she wasn't, Jaydon's sister was off-limits.

Now she was pregnant and in danger. A romantic relationship was out of the question. Which was fine. That wasn't why he'd come for her. He'd known Jaydon, his swim buddy all through BUD/S training, would expect him to find his sister and to keep her safe.

After long months, he finally had found her. He sent up a silent prayer, asking for God's grace and strength to enable him to keep Ava and her unborn child safe from harm.

AVA TWISTED her fingers in her lap, doing her best to ignore Nico's overwhelming presence beside her. Shocking to learn he'd been looking for her all this time. She was grateful for his reassuring presence, but she couldn't help feeling on edge.

Simon was out there, looking for her with the intent to silence her once and for all. Callie, too, which was why she needed to get to the woman she considered a sister.

Because they both knew too much.

She and Callie had been moving from city to city, managing to stay one step ahead of Simon and his goons. She knew Nico would badger her about going to the police, but he didn't understand what she'd done. Only out of necessity, but that wasn't how it would look. No, she couldn't risk having her baby in jail, so she'd done everything possible to stay off Simon's radar. Her goal, and Callie's too, was to stay hidden until she had the baby.

After that, their plan was to slip into Mexico, disappearing forever.

Now that Nico Ramirez had found her, her plan was in jeopardy. Nico would keep looking for her, no matter what. And staying to fight wasn't an option. What could one man do against Simon's empire?

Nothing. Nico would only get hurt.

The way Brent Green had when he'd tried to help four months ago.

Her stomach clenched at the thought of having more blood on her hands. She wouldn't be able to live with herself if Nico died in a vain effort to save her too.

So much death and destruction, and for what? Power and money. It all came down to cold, hard cash. Along with Simon's thirst for revenge.

"Wait! Where are you going?" she asked sharply. Nico

had turned onto the next street, heading several blocks away from the Lizard Lounge. She twisted in her seat, no easy feat, to check out the back window. "Is someone following us?"

"No, you're safe." He glanced at her, his dark brown eyes shimmering with concern. "You need to trust me, Ava. I'm not going to let anything happen to you."

She wanted to trust him, but after so many months of being on the run and in hiding, she couldn't seem to drop her guard. Especially since Nico really had no idea who he was up against. Sure, he was a Navy SEAL the way her brother once was, before Jaydon had been killed by an underwater bomb explosion. But he was still only one man, up against a ruthless band of killers. Her fingers knotted as he went several blocks out of the way before finally turning around at the next block to go back toward the Lizard Lounge.

He pulled into the parking lot, then backed into a spot near the exit. Keeping the car running, he turned toward her. "What does Callie look like? I'll go inside to get her."

She rolled her eyes. "Callie isn't going to go anywhere with a complete stranger. She'll assume you were sent by Simon too. I'll get her."

"No way am I letting you head inside alone." His curt tone irritated her. Partially because she was tired and crabby after being on her feet for nine hours. Her job was that of a bartender, while Callie worked as a waitress. It wasn't a bad job, and she did well with tips. At least, she had before she'd become so noticeably pregnant. Now if she received a great tip, it was likely out of pity.

"One look at you, and she'll run." Ava reached over to lightly touch his arm. His skin was so hot it was a wonder her fingertips didn't blister from the heat. "I'll need to reassure her that you're not with Simon. Just give me a few minutes to talk to her, okay?"

"Fine. We'll go in together," he said with obvious reluctance.

She stared at him for a long moment, then sighed. "Okay, have it your way. But you need to let me take the lead. I don't need you scaring Callie to death. We've only been here in San Bernardino for the past five weeks. We just moved into that apartment." And deep down, she was mad that she had to leave, all because of a moment of weakness.

Why had she contacted Jill? She knew better than to do something so stupid. But her hormones were running amok, and she'd had a breakdown after a particularly brutal day at work. Callie hadn't been home, and she'd allowed herself to wallow in self-pity.

She'd never realized how being isolated from everyone you knew could wear a person down. Even with Callie as her friend, she'd longed for the comforts of home. The people she'd once visited with on a regular basis. Like Jill.

Enough. She'd told herself there was no point in wallowing in regrets. This mess was her fault for falling for Simon in the first place. Not that she ever could have anticipated being on the run for her life when she'd started seeing him.

That she'd be forced to kill another human being to escape.

A wave of nausea hit hard. She ruthlessly shoved the memory aside. Time to move forward. They couldn't stick around San Bernardino for long. She slid out of the passenger seat with all the grace of a baby buffalo, wincing as she stood on her sore and swollen feet. She managed to shut the door behind her and moved toward the front of the restaurant. Nico quickly joined her, slipping his hand beneath her elbow.

"What about Zulu?"

"I left the windows down for her. And I can remotely start the Jeep with the air-conditioning on full blast if this takes longer than it should."

She nodded, impressed with how much he cared for his dog. After her initial fear of the Doberman had faded, she'd realized Nico and Zulu were quite a dynamic pair. And the way Zulu had licked her hand when Nico introduced her had been sweet.

Casting a quick glance around the parking lot, she hurried up to the door. Nico kept pace behind her, reaching around to open the door when she arrived.

A weak blast of air-conditioning hit when she crossed the threshold. She stood there for a moment, searching for Callie. The girl had dark hair that had been resistant to hair dye, making it harder for her to escape Simon's notice. Callie had cut it short, but even that didn't alter her appearance much.

"How come you weren't wearing one of those uniforms?" Nico asked in a low voice.

"I was, but I changed." The uniform he mentioned was a white, off-the-shoulder peasant blouse with a brightly colored skirt. Even the female bartenders were forced to wear them, which seemed silly to her. But it was a job, and Pedro, the boss, hadn't asked many questions other than how soon she and Callie could start working.

Their answer? Immediately.

"Where is she?" Nico asked, his tone laced with impatience. "We need to get out of here."

"I don't see her." Which was strange as the tables were more than half full. Normally, Callie would be hustling back and forth, chatting with her customers. Her friend was a great waitress. Better than she was a bartender, that was for sure.

Ava wove through the tables, taking care not to bump into anyone as she went. When she reached the corner of the bar, she waited to catch Ramon's eye. "Where's Callie?"

"No idea." Ramon, her fellow bartender, was barely twenty-one and treated her as if she were eighty rather than thirty-two. "I think Pedro is looking for her too."

A chill snaked down her spine. Why would Pedro be looking for her? Callie's shift didn't end for another hour yet.

"Come on, we need to hurry," Nico said.

"I'm trying," she snapped. Then she took a deep breath. He was probably worried about Zulu being in the car. Thankfully, the sun was down, but still, the heat could still be oppressive. She headed around the bar toward the back room where Pedro, the owner and manager, had a tiny office, when he came rushing toward her.

"Renee! Where is Callie?" He was short, his dark hair liberally laced with gray. "Did she go home with you?"

The chill coalesced to ice. "No. She's not with me. How long has she been gone?" She glanced back at Nico. He'd taken an alternate route, so they wouldn't have passed Callie along the way.

"Ten or fifteen minutes," Pedro said. "She took her break but didn't come back. I thought maybe she went to see you." Pedro flushed, glancing at her stomach. "I told myself the baby might have come early."

"I'm fine, and I haven't seen her." She pushed past Pedro to check the small break area for herself.

The small round table tucked into the corner of the supply room was empty.

She swallowed hard and turned to face Nico. "Callie wouldn't take off like this, not without a good reason. She's a good worker."

"You think Simon's men found her?" Nico asked, his expression grave.

She closed her eyes, leaned against him, and nodded. And the worst part was that if Simon had Callie, he wouldn't hesitate to use her as bait to get to her.

And their unborn child.

# CHAPTER TWO

"Simon might have kidnapped Callie." Ava's fear was palpable as she gripped his arm tightly. "We need to head back to the apartment just to be sure."

That was the last place Nico wanted to go, but he also needed to get Ava out of there, so he nodded and put his hand over hers. "We'll check things out, okay?"

She gave a terse nod and followed as he led her through the restaurant. Customers eyed them curiously, but he ignored them.

Outside, he urged Ava toward the Jeep. Using the key fob, he remotely started the vehicle, then opened the passenger door for her. Seconds later, they were on the road.

"Maybe Callie saw something that scared her," Ava said, raking her hand through her curls. "You took a circuitous route to the restaurant; we never would have seen her if she walked back."

He was both touched and annoyed by her concern for Callie. Ava's loyalty was admirable, but he wanted her to be safe. And heading back to the apartment wasn't the way to do that. Not with the bald biker dude watching the place.

Ava wouldn't like it, but he'd need to leave her and Zulu in the Jeep while he went to check the apartment for Callie. He didn't care if Callie might be frightened by his presence, all that mattered was getting her safely out of there. The strange guy lingering near the building only reinforced his belief that the place was being watched.

This time, Ava didn't protest when he took an indirect route back to the apartment. But when he pulled over to park several blocks away, in a different location than last time, she frowned. "Can't you get any closer?"

"I can, but I won't." He turned in his seat to face her. "I need to go in alone, Ava." She immediately opened her mouth to argue, but he held up his hand. "I know you're worried about Callie's reaction to a stranger, but there was a guy watching the place, remember? I can get in and out of there without him seeing me."

"Callie will scream and fight," Ava warned.

"Tell me something only the two of you know." He held her gaze for a long moment. "Something that will reassure her that I'm not going to hurt her."

Ava hesitated, then thankfully capitulated. "The two names I've picked out for the baby are Jaydon for a boy and Jayne with a *y* for a girl."

He nodded slowly. "Jaydon would be thrilled to know you are naming your child after him."

She nodded and swiped at her eyes. "Stupid hormones," she muttered. "I seem to cry at everything these days."

"It's natural, don't worry about it." He pushed open his car door. "I'm bringing Zulu up front with you. That way she'll protect you if anyone tries to get inside the car."

"Uh, okay." She seemed hesitant, but once Zulu was sitting in the driver's seat, she relaxed back against the seat cushion. "As long as she doesn't bite me, we're good."

"She won't bite you, but she will go after and bite a bad guy." He smiled. "I'll be back as soon as possible."

"Okay." For once, Ava didn't argue. He wanted to believe that was because she trusted him, but he felt it was more sheer exhaustion holding her back.

Either way, he was relieved to be on his own. Nico slipped into the shadows, thankful that many of the street-lights were out in this area of the city. He knew how to move silently through the night and easily steered clear of the area where he'd seen the man lurking just twenty minutes ago.

Yet as he moved toward the apartment building, he noticed the tough-looking lurker wasn't there. He didn't doubt the guy had simply moved locations.

Or maybe he'd gotten his hands on Callie.

He hated the idea of Ava's friend being in danger. If he could get her out of the apartment, he would. But if Callie wasn't there, he would absolutely get Ava far away from this place.

Crouching at the base of a tree across from the back door of the apartment building, he scoured the area. Just as he was about to make his move, two men came out the back door. They were Hispanic, like Nico, but heavily tattooed. And not the professional type of tattoo, more like the self-made-while-in-jail kind of ink.

The two men stood for a moment speaking in low voices. He understood Spanish well enough to understand they were planning their next drug buy.

More proof that Ava and Callie shouldn't be living in a place like this. Once they moved away, Nico came out of hiding. He didn't carry his weapon in hand, mostly because he didn't want to scare Callie, but he was armed with both his Sig Sauer and the MK 3 knife the SEALs favored.

He crossed to the back door and slipped inside. There, he hugged the wall as he crept toward Ava and Callie's apartment. As he got closer, he froze, realizing the door was hanging ajar.

Not good. Ava had closed and locked it when they left.

Slipping the Sig from its holster, he moved forward, mentally braced for an attack. Using his foot, he pushed the door open, then took a quick glance inside.

The main living space appeared empty. He silently moved inside, clearing the back of the door before closing it. Then he made his way to the small bedroom and bathroom. There were two twin beds, indicating the girls shared a room.

The apartment was empty, and from what he could tell, there were no signs of a struggle. Either Callie had been caught just as she'd unlocked the door or she went without a fight, likely held at gunpoint.

There was nothing more he could do, so he left as silently as he'd come. He took a moment to close the door, then headed to the back door.

The two guys were back, along with three others who looked similar as far as the inexpert tattoos and the way they were dressed. It was difficult to watch a drug buy going on right outside the door without doing anything to stop it, but he didn't dare draw their attention. In his experience, it wouldn't take much to convince any of these guys to describe him to Simon's men for a measly fifty bucks. Or less, whatever they'd need for their next fix.

Once the drug buy had been completed, the men scattered like the rats they were. Nico slipped through the door and melted into the shadows.

It didn't take him long to make his way back to the Jeep.

When he was close enough to see that Ava and Zulu appeared unharmed, he began to relax.

But when Ava saw him there, alone, her expression crumpled. "No Callie?"

"I'm afraid not." He took a moment to put Zulu in the back crate area. When he slid into the driver's seat, he quickly started the car. "The apartment door wasn't closed all the way, so someone had been there, but I didn't see a sign of a struggle." He glanced at Ava. "Does anyone else have a key?"

"The building manager has a master." Ava looked as if she might burst into tears again. "It doesn't make sense, though, that the door was open. I'm sure Callie was taken from the restaurant. I guess someone could have taken her key to access the apartment to find me."

It was an angle he hadn't considered. "Does Callie have a phone?"

"We both have cheap, disposable phones." She wiped at her eyes again. "I'll try calling her."

He nodded and pulled out onto the street. It was clear Ava's call went unanswered when she tucked the phone into her oversized bag she carried across her chest. "We have to find her, Nico. Before Simon hurts her."

*Or worse*, he thought grimly. If Simon was as bad as Ava had claimed, there was a strong possibility Callie wouldn't survive the night. As much as that thought bothered him, his primary concern was Ava and her baby. "Right now, we need to find a safe place to stay."

"Here in San Bernardino, right?" Ava persisted. "We can't just leave without doing more to find Callie."

He didn't know how they were going to find the missing woman without anything to go on. Then a thought hit him. "Does the Lizard Lounge have security cameras?"

"I think so, at least on the front of the building." She grimaced. "I never noticed if Pedro posted any out back."

"Okay, I'll try to convince Pedro to show me his video. But we need to get you settled first." He cast a sideways glance at her. "I can tell your feet are killing you."

"That's something all pregnant women suffer from, it's no big deal." She rested her hands on her belly. "I'm not going to fall apart just because I have to walk. I've been walking back and forth to work for weeks, and that was after working a nine-hour shift."

He hid a wince. Nine hours on her feet? Ugh. "I never meant to insinuate you're helpless, I'm only trying to ease your discomfort." He knew he was being a bit overprotective, but she was pregnant, and he couldn't risk anything bad happening to her or the baby. "Humor me, okay? I'll feel better once you're able to get some rest."

"Go back to the Lizard Lounge first," she insisted. "Pedro won't let you see the video, but he'll probably let me look at it. He knows me and was genuinely concerned about Callie going missing."

Probably only because he needed someone to wait tables, but Nico didn't voice his thought. He drove through the city, trying to think of a compromise. Finally, he decided the sooner he checked the video feed with Ava's help, the sooner he could get out of town.

"Okay, we'll return to the Lizard Lounge." He didn't love the idea, but he hoped enough time had passed that Simon's men wouldn't backtrack to find them there. "Is there a back door to the place? I don't want to go in through the front."

"Yes, it's right off the kitchen." Ava reached over to pat his arm. "Thanks, Nico. It means a lot to me that you're willing to help find Callie."

He nodded, managing a smile while hoping this side trip wasn't a terrible mistake. The only good thing was that if there was nothing on the video showing Callie getting kidnapped, then he'd work to convince Ava they needed to get out of town ASAP.

And if she was seen being taken away against her will? He'd call his cop buddy Bryce Flynn to let him take over the investigation. This wasn't in Bryce's jurisdiction, but he didn't doubt Flynn could get someone within the San Bernardino police department to take him seriously.

Then he could focus on keeping Ava safe and getting to the bottom of why she didn't feel like she could go to the police for help.

Envisioning the map of the area in his mind, he pulled over to a secluded spot roughly two blocks from the back of the restaurant. He wanted to convince Ava to stay in the car, but he knew she was right about Pedro being more likely to share the video with her than with him.

He released the back hatch so Zulu could jump out. He felt bad for the Doberman, she'd been cooped up for most of the day. First by his driving here, then when he'd made her stay silent beside him while he watched the apartment building.

"I'll let you burn off some steam later, girl, okay?" He connected the leash to her collar, then turned to Ava. "Stay behind me, okay?"

"I know the drill."

Maybe it was his imagination, but she seemed to be less worried and anxious about being found by Simon's thugs. He led the way toward the back of the restaurant, then stopped abruptly when a dark-haired man wearing an apron tied around his waist came out, lugging a bag of garbage.

The man never glanced at them, he simply tossed the garbage into the dumpster and went back inside.

"That was Eddie," Ava said in a hushed tone. "He's the restaurant dishwasher. Nice guy but doesn't speak much English."

He nodded, then continued moving forward. Soon they were inside the rear portion of the restaurant. Without hesitation, Ava turned into Pedro's office.

"Renee. What are you doing here?" Pedro asked in surprise.

"Callie isn't at the apartment, and I'm very worried about her." She took a step closer. "Pedro, will you please show me and my friend Nico your surveillance videos? We want to see if Callie left on her own or if someone forced her."

Pedro's gaze narrowed as he glanced between Nico and Ava. "Fine." He punched several keys on his computer, then gestured at it. "I went back to the last time I saw Callie."

"Gracias, Pedro." Ava stepped back to give the older man room to get out from behind the desk. The small office was crowded with three people, one pregnant, and the dog. Ava took a seat behind Pedro's desk and began running the video. Nico stood beside her, watching the screen intently.

Fifteen minutes passed before a slender woman with short, dark hair wearing the restaurant uniform stepped outside. "That's Callie," Ava said.

He nodded and watched as the video continued to play. Callie walked toward one of the outdoor tables, then abruptly stopped when a man stepped forward. They appeared to talk for a minute, then they walked off, together, disappearing from view.

"That doesn't make sense," Ava said with a frown. "Callie wouldn't go off in the middle of her shift."

"Could she have a boyfriend she didn't tell you about?"

"No, she'd have told me." Ava glanced up at him. "There's a server here she liked, his name is Ricardo, but that guy wasn't him. Ricardo is young, late-twenties, the same age as Callie. That guy was at least thirty-five."

"Play it again, slower," Nico directed.

Ava went back to the beginning and played the video again at a much slower speed. The image quality wasn't great, but when the stranger stepped forward, he thought he saw something in the man's hand. "Stop." Ava hit the pause key. He pointed to the screen. "It looks like he has a gun."

She backed it up and played that section of the video again. This time, Nico could see the nose of the gun being pressed to Callie's side. The guy had been skilled enough to make it look as if their meeting was a casual thing between friends.

"I knew it," Ava whispered. "I knew Callie wouldn't go with him willingly."

He hated to admit she was right. The guy with the gun hadn't looked directly at the cameras, but they did have a profile view. It might be enough to run through a facial recognition software program. He didn't have that ability, but Bryce would.

With a sinking sensation in his gut, Nico realized he and Ava wouldn't be leaving San Bernardino anytime soon.

---

WATCHING Callie being taken away at gunpoint had shaken her badly. Ava suddenly realized that if not for Nico showing up when he did, she would be with Callie too.

There was no doubt in her mind the gunman had gone to the apartment to get her.

"Ask Pedro if he'll give us a copy of this video," Nico said, breaking in to her troubled thoughts. "But quickly. We need to get out of here."

"Pedro?" Ava called. The owner of the restaurant hurried back. "We need a copy of this. It proves Callie was taken against her will."

Pedro made the sign of the cross, then edged past Ava to make the copy.

"Thank you, Pedro." She took the small CD and handed it to Nico.

The older man frowned and stared at Nico. "Keep Renee and her baby safe from harm, amigo."

"I promise," Nico agreed.

Ava felt bad leaving Pedro in the lurch, the poor guy had just lost two employees in a matter of hours. She gave him a brief hug, then quickly followed Nico outside.

Zulu was amazingly quiet as they made their way back to the Jeep. Ava didn't notice her sore feet until she took her usual place in the passenger seat. She managed not to moan and schooled her features to hide her relief at being able to sit.

Nico was acting as if she needed to be bubble wrapped and set up on a shelf somewhere until her baby was born. And while she looked forward to getting some rest, she couldn't ignore the fact that the woman who'd also escaped Simon's goons was now back in danger.

The baby kicked and rolled, bringing a reluctant smile to her face. It was impossible to dwell on the negative while carrying the promise of a new life inside your womb. Ava did her best to draw in a deep breath, letting it out slowly.

She'd read enough to know that stress wasn't good for a baby.

Yet if that was true, this poor baby was doomed as she'd been under stress for most of her pregnancy.

"Is something wrong? Are you feeling ill?" Nico asked urgently. "Do you need to see a doctor?"

"I'm fine. Just trying to relax." Truth be told, she was overdue for a doctor's appointment. She'd found a free clinic here in San Bernardino, but she hadn't been able to get in until next week.

Now that visit likely wouldn't happen. She took another slow, deep breath. Women had been giving birth for years, seeing a doctor every month, then every few weeks wasn't necessarily a requirement. She ate healthy food and took her prenatal vitamins. All a doctor would do is ask how she felt and check her vital signs.

At least, that's all the previous doctors had done when she'd managed to get in to see someone. One very helpful doctor had counseled her that if she thought she was in labor, she should go to the nearest emergency room. There were laws that prevented hospitals from discharging a woman in labor just because she didn't have insurance. She'd been grateful for the advice.

"I'll find us a motel," Nico said. "You need to lie down with your feet up."

Stretching out with her feet up sounded like such a luxury and made her feel even more guilty about Callie. The baby kicked again, and she put her hand over the spot where the little foot had poked her. "Can we stay in the area?"

Nico hesitated, sighed, then nodded. "I'll find something on the outskirts of town, okay?"

"Thanks." She shifted in her seat. "I wish we had a

computer so we could watch the video again. Maybe we can get a clue about where the gunman took Callie."

"I have a computer," Nico said. "But I'd prefer to give the video to a cop friend of mine. He'll be able to use software to find an ID of the guy who took her."

She immediately stiffened. "No cops, Nico. I told you that."

"Listen, Ava, if we don't call the cops, there's zero chance that Callie will survive this. You're in over your head here. I get you're afraid, but you need to let the police handle Simon."

"No cops," she repeated. A wave of desperation hit hard. "Please, Nico. I'm begging you. No cops."

He shot her an incredulous glance, then looked away. "Fine. I won't do anything, yet."

She didn't find his comment at all reassuring. An uncomfortable silence fell between them as he used his smartphone to find a reasonably priced motel.

After pulling up to the main doors, he threw the gearshift into park and turned to face her. "Stay here with Zulu. I'll get us a room."

"One room?" She frowned. Did Nico think she was the type of woman to sleep around just because she was pregnant? Because she wasn't. She'd gone with Simon willingly, sure. They'd hugged, kissed, and generally made out. But when it came time to go all the way, she'd tried to say no.

Simon hadn't taken no for an answer.

Even worse, he'd tried to strangle her into submission. She'd had the bruises around her neck to prove it.

It was the impetus she'd needed to get away from him for good.

She slammed the door on those memories. She'd come to love her unborn child and knew the baby was an innocent blessing. Yet she also knew she couldn't let Simon anywhere near the infant.

Hence her plan to flee the country as soon as the baby was born.

"Connecting rooms," Nico swiftly clarified as if reading her mind. "But I need you to keep the connecting door unlocked, okay?"

"Okay." She managed a smile. "Thanks."

Nico hurried inside, returning amazingly quickly with two keycards. "We're all set. Rooms fourteen and fifteen at the end of the row."

She nodded, hoping the rooms weren't roach-infested the way the apartment had been. Those creepy-crawlies had been the most difficult thing for her to deal with. Up until getting involved with Simon, she'd never had to worry about that.

A wave of self-reproach hit hard. Why had she gone out with him?

Why had she readily jumped on the back of his motorcycle without a second thought?

Why hadn't she left him sooner?

"Ava?" Nico's deep, husky voice drew her from her thoughts. "Are you sure you're feeling okay?"

No, she wasn't sure of anything. But falling apart wouldn't help. She needed to be strong. For the baby's sake. "Yes." She realized he'd parked the car several spots away from their two rooms. Nico jumped out, reached for her backpack, then let Zulu out of the back hatch. Moving slowly, she pushed open the door and climbed out of the Jeep.

"Do you have a preference?" He held up the two key cards.

"The one without roaches," she said wearily.

"The manager assured me they spray on a regular basis," Nico said. He unlocked the first door and pushed it open. She peered inside, relieved to see it looked and smelled relatively clean.

Nico and Zulu followed her inside. Nico dropped her backpack onto the bed, then crossed over to unlock the connecting doors. "Give me a few minutes, okay? I need to let Zulu out to do her thing."

"That's fine." She sat on the bed, swung her feet up, and leaned against the headboard. She breathed out a sigh, then gasped as Nico came over to pick up the second pillow. "Here, you need to be comfortable."

"I am." She was surprised by his sweet gesture. Yet she also knew Nico's kindness was centered on the fact that she was Jaydon's younger sister. Nothing more. Especially now that she was pregnant with another man's baby. Not just any man's.

The mastermind behind the Desert Death Rays biker gang.

"I'll be back soon." He left, taking Zulu with him. She'd begun to think of the sleek, black Doberman as a shadow. Her experience was with small dogs who never seemed to stop barking.

Her eyelids drifted closed as she gave up fighting against the overwhelming exhaustion. Before becoming pregnant, she'd always been full of energy, to the point she'd often had trouble falling asleep.

Not anymore. Aside from the nausea, she'd known by the sheer exhaustion that she was expecting. Never in her life had she felt as tired as she had over those past few months. Running and hiding from Simon certainly didn't help.

Relaxing into the pillows, she sighed. All she needed was a brief reprieve.

A hand on her arm brought her wide awake in a heartbeat. The knife blade was in her hand before she could blink. But as she lashed out, Nico caught her wrist.

"Whoa, what's wrong?"

She stared at him for a moment, realizing she'd betrayed her deepest fear of being attacked. "You startled me."

"And that causes you to lash out with a knife?" He sounded incredulous, as if he didn't carry both a knife and a gun. "Where did you hide it anyway?"

"The side pocket of my bag." She stared at him intently, but he didn't back down. "I'm sorry, but you shouldn't sneak up on me. After all, Jaydon is the one who taught me how to use a knife." And a gun, but she didn't own one of those.

"I'm surprised you didn't pull a knife when I caught up with you outside the apartment." He let go of her wrist and took a step back. "We're safe here, but I think it's time for you to fill me in on exactly what's been going on."

She swallowed hard. "Tomorrow."

"No, tonight." He pulled the single chair in the room closer to the bed. "Start at the beginning."

She shook her head helplessly. She didn't want to do this. Didn't want to tell the handsome guy she'd secretly crushed on just how foolish she'd been.

Once Nico knew the truth about her naïvete and how she'd killed a man, he'd never look at her the same way again.

The sweet compassion in his eyes would turn to hard contempt.

AND HONESTLY, she knew deep down she deserved it.

# CHAPTER THREE

Ava slept with a knife. Nico had known things must have been difficult for her, but narrowly missing being stabbed in the chest made him realize he'd underestimated what she'd endured.

No woman should be made to feel unsafe. Especially not at nearly eight months pregnant.

Granted, he was relieved Jaydon had taught her to protect herself. Although he couldn't help but wonder if that was the case, then why was Simon still a threat. She should have just stabbed him in the chest and been done with it.

"Please, Ava." He reached out to cradle her hand between his. "Whatever happened, you don't have to worry. I promise it will be okay."

"Don't make promises you can't keep." The words were razor sharp. "There's a reason I can't go to the police."

A warning chill snaked down his spine. "Please tell me."

She closed her eyes and looked away. She seemed to gather herself before turning back to him. "You saw that guy outside the apartment building, right?"

"Yes." He'd asked her to start at the beginning but decided against interrupting. It was her story to tell in any way she chose.

"Did you see any of his tattoos? I couldn't see it, but I thought he had something on his bicep."

"He did. The letters DDR above skull and crossbones." He shrugged. "Not very original if you ask me."

Her gaze darted to the Navy SEAL tattoo on his arm for a moment. "The DDR stands for Desert Death Rays. They're a motorcycle gang."

"Okay." It made sense, remembering the motorcycle boots. "Are you saying Simon is involved with them?"

"He's the leader. Oh, and while they might have started out small, his goal is for their gang to become as well known and as fearsome as the Hell's Angels."

Nico was getting a bad feeling about this. "You're saying they're dangerous."

"Yes." She pulled her hand from his and looked away. "It's my fault, Nico. I was bored, cleaning teeth all day, every day as a dental hygienist wasn't enough. I don't know why I thought Simon was cool, his motorcycle romantic. But I went with him willingly. And it was only once I became exposed to the others and realized what they were doing that I knew I'd made a big mistake."

"Ava, just because you dated the guy doesn't make you a criminal too," he protested.

She turned to glare at him. "Let me finish. It's more than that." She took a moment to smooth her hands over her belly as if trying to remain calm. He felt bad for making her relive all this, but he needed to know what they were up against. After a full minute, she said, "I should have left Simon sooner. The minute I resisted, he turned violent. You said you know about my being at the woman's shelter run by

Charlotte." Her hands went up to her throat for a moment, then dropped back down to her belly again.

"Simon found you there?"

"Yes. I saw one of his motorcycle goons outside the shelter and knew that my staying there would put them all in danger." She licked her lips. "Simon made it clear he wants me back."

"Because of the baby?"

"Not at first. I only found out I was pregnant after I left the shelter." She finally turned to look at him. "Simon was determined to make me pay because I killed one of his men. A man named Banjo."

He squelched a flash of annoyance. Not because she had killed a guy but because it had been keeping her from going to the police. "Ava, killing a man in self-defense is nothing to be worried about. No judge or jury is going to come down on you for lashing out at some guy to escape being held against your will by a motorcycle gang."

"You don't know what you're talking about," she scoffed. She rummaged in her bag and brought out a brown five-by-eight-inch envelope. She thrust it at him. "See for yourself. Oh, and let's not forget that I went with Simon willingly. That our faces are on dozens of gas station cameras all over Los Angeles. Who on earth will believe he held me against my will, that he tried to strangle me, and forced me . . ." She trailed off, her hands returning to her abdomen.

Battling fury laced with dread, he slid the glossy photos from the envelope. There were only two, but they were very clear. In one photo, a biker had a hand on Ava's arm, and the two seemed to be talking. The next photo, Ava was holding a knife that was embedded in the guy's neck.

The images surely didn't paint the true picture. He

shoved them back into the envelope. "How do you know Banjo died?"

"The way the blood gushed out of the wound in an arch, I knew I'd hit his carotid artery." Her voice was dull. "I only had seconds to escape, and the way Banjo was holding on to my arm, I knew he'd keep me there until Simon showed up. Or he'd drag me back to Simon. He easily outweighed me by a hundred pounds. I carried on a pleasant conversation long enough to get the knife in my hand, then stabbed him when he wasn't expecting it. Once he slid to the ground, I took off running without looking back."

"It's still self-defense," he said, although he could see how the photos could be misinterpreted. "I truly believe we need to take this all to the police. Explain what happened and go from there."

"No. I'm not having my baby in jail." Ava tipped her chin up defiantly. "If you want to help me find Callie, and to help me stay hidden until after I have the baby, fine. I'll accept your help. But if you insist on getting the police involved, I'm out of here."

He could tell she was dead serious, and while he still believed she'd be found innocent of wrongdoing, he knew the wheels of justice moved slowly. Depending on the situation, she may not be granted bail. And if that was the case, he knew having a baby in jail was a definite possibility. "Okay, we'll stay off-grid for now. But, Ava, I need you to be honest with me from now on. Is there anything else I need to know?"

"Isn't that enough?" she asked wearily. "Simon knows he can hold those photographs against me. And now that he has Callie?" She grimaced. "I'm afraid he'll use her to get to me."

*Over his dead body*, Nico thought. *Simon's not his*, he silently amended. "Where is Simon's motorcycle headquarters?"

"In Los Angeles."

"And how does Callie fit in?"

"She was with one of the other biker dudes, a guy named Otto, but managed to escape. I was heading back to find her when she'd slipped away too. We left together and since then have stayed close." She frowned. "I'm not sure how Simon knew we ended up together. Although maybe he assumed we escaped together since we both got out of there about the same time."

Ava's pale face tugged at his heart. "Okay, that's enough for now. You need to get some rest."

Her hand shot out to grasp his. "You need to promise me you won't talk to your cop friend."

"I promise." He'd follow her wishes, at least for now. "Get some rest, Ava. You need to take care of yourself. For little Jaydon's sake."

"Jayne," she corrected. "I think the baby is a girl."

"Whether you have a girl or boy, the baby will be a blessing from God." He smiled as he rose. Zulu jumped to her feet too. "Sleep well, Ava. You're safe here."

"Thanks." A hint of uncertainty shadowed her gaze. As if she wasn't sure what to make of him.

Had she expected him to be upset at what she'd done? Ridiculous. No matter how the photos looked, he knew Ava wouldn't have killed a man unless her life was in danger. And being held by Simon, whatever his last name was these days, was clearly putting her at risk.

He only hoped he'd get a chance to take Simon out of the game very soon. He wouldn't outright kill the guy unless he had to, not that he'd lose any sleep over it. He'd settle for having him arrested and tossed in jail for the rest of his life.

"Come, Zulu." He led the Doberman through the connecting doors. After taking a few moments to use the bathroom, he took the K9 out one last time. When he returned, he was relieved to see that Ava had left her side of the connecting door open an inch for easy access between their rooms.

Anyone trying to hurt her would have to go through him and Zulu. "Guard, Zulu," he said to the Doberman. He pointed at the spot in front of the connecting door and near the side of his bed. "Guard Ava."

Zulu stretched out on the floor, looking up at him for a moment before lowering her head down between her paws.

"Good girl," he murmured, sitting on the edge of the bed. He'd planned to call his teammates to let them know he'd found Ava, but he hesitated now. Would Ava see that as breaking his promise? He grimaced and rubbed the back of his neck.

Dallas had become a cop, but the other guys weren't in law enforcement. Although they'd each played key roles in bringing a variety of criminals to justice over the past several months. Exactly why he'd love to have their help now.

Nico decided to wait until tomorrow. He wanted to be truthful with Ava, so he wouldn't make the call yet.

But he needed to do so soon. Their entire SEAL team had been concerned about Ava's well-being for months now. They'd be relieved to know she was safe with him.

Nico closed his eyes and did his best to place his worries in God's hands. Praying had always helped, even during the most dangerous op. Including that last one, when Jaydon had died.

The entire team had been injured. But they were all doing well now, and that was all because of God's grace.

He had no doubt he'd find a way to get Ava out of trouble too. Simon and his motorcycle gang, the Desert Death Rays, couldn't stand up against a group of Navy SEALs and their K9 partners. Even with their various injuries—Mason's deafness in one ear, Kaleb's reconstructed knee, Hudd's loss of one eye and debilitating headaches, Dawson with his multiple abdominal surgeries, Dallas with his injured shoulder, and his own ruptured Achilles tendon—they were a force to be reckoned with.

*Soon*, he thought with satisfaction. Ava would be safe from harm and fear of imprisonment very soon.

Yet the nagging thought that lingered as he drifted off to sleep was what he'd do with the rest of his life once this mission was over.

---

AVA SLEPT IN SPURTS, often having to change positions to be comfortable and getting up to use the bathroom. Despite how tired she was, she couldn't help but marvel at how Nico had taken the news about how she'd killed Banjo. She'd expected him to be revolted by what she'd done.

Instead, he'd been his usual sweet, kind self. Oh, she knew full well he'd offered his support out of loyalty to Jaydon. Even going as far as to deem her actions self-defense. And that her baby was a blessing from God.

As much as she appreciated his acceptance of what she'd done, she could tell he'd continue to pressure her about going to the police.

That was a nonstarter, and the sooner he realized that fact, the better.

Things would be easier if it wasn't for Callie. She was worried about the woman she'd cared for like a sister. Simon's biker goons had taken her, and it was only a matter of time before they reached out to Ava. She was charging her disposable phone specifically for that purpose.

Once she would have prayed for Callie's safety. But that was before Simon.

Before she'd been exposed to pure evil.

And well before she'd broken one of the Lord's Ten Commandments.

*Thou shalt not kill.*

She squeezed her eyes shut, tears leaking down her cheeks. The awful memory haunted her still, sometimes waking her from a deep sleep, her heart pounding in terror. In her dreams, she didn't escape but was captured by Simon, feeling his large, broad hands closing around her throat and cutting off her breathing.

Until she died.

The worst part of her situation was that if she could go back to that fateful night to start over, she'd do the same thing again. Because she'd known it was only a matter of time before Simon killed her.

Yet Banjo had been the one to die. Not Simon. It bothered her that if she could go back, she might be tempted to stab Simon rather than sneak away while he was sleeping.

*Please forgive me.*

The silent plea helped ease the tightness in her chest. She told herself it was because Nico and Zulu were staying in the room next door.

But maybe God hadn't given up on her yet either.

She finally relaxed enough to fall back asleep. Thankfully, the nightmare with Simon didn't return. But she was woken by a strange noise. Not a loud sound, but something low and rumbling. It took a moment for her to identify the source.

Zulu growling.

Instantly, she sat bolt upright, swinging her legs over the edge of the bed. She wore a nightgown and quickly pulled it down to cover herself. She slipped her feet into her flat sandals, then reached for her bag, her fingers closing around the knife she always kept readily accessible in the side pocket.

Something was wrong. In the few hours she'd spent with Zulu, the animal never barked and had only growled when they'd first met.

"Ava?" Nico's voice was barely a whisper, his large shadow crossing through the open doorway between their rooms. "I need you to hide in the bathroom. Curl up in the bathtub."

"Why? What's happening?" she whispered, her imagination going into overdrive as she feared the worst. "Is Simon out there?"

"I don't know, but I plan to find out." Now that her eyes had adjusted to the dim light, she could see he held his gun in his hand. The thought of Nico shooting someone because of her made her feel sick to her stomach. He held her gaze for a moment. "Stay in the bathroom until I come for you."

"Wait." She grasped his arm. "Can't we just sneak away?"

"If we can, we will." He surprised her by raising her hand to his mouth for a kiss before releasing her. "Stay safe, Ava. Protect yourself and your baby."

She nodded and hurried into the bathroom, closing the door behind her. As she was stepping over the edge of the bathtub, being careful not to slip and fall, she heard Nico say, "Guard, Zulu. Guard Ava."

*No!* The silent scream lodged in the back of her throat. She didn't want Nico to put Zulu in harm's way. Once she managed to get inside the bathtub, she carefully lowered herself and stretched out as much as possible, keeping her belly pressed against the edge of the tub for protection. Then she propped herself up on one elbow so she could see over the edge of the tub. She stared at the closed door, the knife still in her hand.

It wouldn't be the first time she'd used it; clearly, she'd done so before. But she desperately wished it would be the last.

Why wouldn't Simon just leave her alone?

Stupid, evil revenge.

The seconds seemed to pass by with excruciating slowness. She strained to listen, but she couldn't hear anything. Maybe that was a good thing because she'd hear the shots if Nico was forced to use his gun.

*Please, Lord, don't put him in a position where he needs to kill someone!*

Bad enough she had that guilt weighing on her, there was no reason to add a similar burden to Nico.

Yet she knew Nico wouldn't hesitate to do what was necessary. If Simon were smart, and if he knew about Nico and the other Navy SEALs, he'd leave her alone.

Wait, how did Simon find them there? He couldn't possibly know anything about Nico helping her. The bald guy she assumed was one of Simon's biker dudes hadn't seen them.

Had he?

No. Impossible. Even if he had, there's no way he could have tracked them there. Disposable phones were untraceable, or so Simon had always claimed. It was the reason he and his biker buddies exclusively used disposable phones. And she was certain that guy had been waiting for his biker pals to show up, maybe after they'd taken Callie.

Poor Callie. She shivered. She hated to imagine what the woman was suffering at the hands of the Desert Death Rays. The good news was that Callie couldn't tell Simon where she and Nico were because she didn't know about Nico.

No one from Simon's stupid biker gang did. And she'd desperately hoped and prayed it stayed that way.

A muffled trilling sound came from the other room.

Her phone! She lifted her head up over the edge of the bathtub, wondering if she had enough time to grab it. No. It would be a foolish risk. Yet she couldn't help but think that Simon was calling her. Likely after forcing Callie to give up her phone.

It wasn't easy, but she stayed within the relative safety of the bathtub. She rested her forehead against the porcelain, forcing herself to take slow, calming breaths.

The phone stopped ringing, but then she heard a loud thud. So much for calming breaths. Every muscle in her body tightened with fear, especially when Zulu began to growl again.

Simon could be making his way inside the motel room right now! She knew he carried a gun, and he'd shoot the dog before it could attack him.

But then suddenly the door opened, and Nico stood there. His dark hair was damp with sweat, his expression appearing to be carved in stone. He raked a quick gaze over her, then offered his hand. "Are you okay?"

She managed a nod.

"Good. Let's go."

"Wh—what happened?" She allowed him to help her up, leaning on Nico's strength as she stepped out of the bathtub. The urge to throw herself into his arms was difficult to ignore. Ridiculous, as she was pregnant with another man's child.

Nico's loyalty to her dead brother would only go so far. She would not allow herself to lose her heart over him.

"Later. Time to move."

She was acutely self-conscious of the fact that she wore nothing but her nightgown, although it covered pretty much the same territory as her sundress. Clearly there was no time to change into something else. Nico had her backpack slung over his shoulder, along with a dark-colored duffel bag that must have contained his gear and stuff for Zulu, too, she imagined.

He led her out through his door, taking a moment to glance both ways before edging out farther. The Jeep was in the same spot where he'd left it, but she gaped when she saw two biker dudes stretched out on the ground, unmoving. One of them had a gun lying about three feet from his body.

Two of them! She stared incredulously. Nico had taken out two of Simon's guys!

"Hurry." Nico's curt tone had her quickening her pace to reach the Jeep. She wondered if the police were on their way, the sounds of Nico fighting those men must have caused someone to call the authorities. She hastily climbed into the passenger seat. No easy task with her bag getting in the way. She irritably pushed it aside and sat, reaching for the seatbelt. The moment Nico had Zulu settled in the back, he joined her up front.

Seconds later, they were speeding away from the motel. They were safe. For now. But Callie wasn't. She mentally smacked herself for her lapse. "Nico, wait. My phone." She grabbed his arm. "I heard it ringing while I was in the bathroom. I'm sure the caller was either Simon or Callie."

"I agree, it's likely they took Callie's phone to connect with you, but we have to leave it behind," Nico said.

"But how else am I going to get in touch with Callie?" She couldn't just leave the girl in Simon's clutches. She just couldn't!

"We'll think of something. Once we're safe." He reached up to wipe his forehead. His fingers came away dark with blood.

"You're hurt." She tightened her grip on his arm, for her sake more than anything. The thought of Nico being hurt made her dizzy with fear and worry. She pulled herself together with an effort. "We need to stop at a drug store for bandages."

"I'm fine. It's just a scratch." He didn't move as if he were in pain, but she knew head injuries could be serious. "We need to figure out how they found us."

"Through my phone?" She shivered again, realizing how precarious their position had been.

"Doubtful, but we have to consider all angles."

She swallowed hard and nodded. She fell silent, grimly acknowledging that if Nico hadn't had Zulu to alert them, the night could have ended very differently.

With one or both of them dead.

# CHAPTER FOUR

Driving away from the motel was a relief, but Nico felt it was short-lived. Somehow, his vehicle must have been compromised, but until they were far away from the crime scene, he couldn't take the time to check it for a GPS tracking device.

It seemed far-fetched to think the one guy they'd seen lurking outside the apartment had figured out which vehicle was his. But maybe there had been other Desert Death Rays he hadn't noticed? He'd been out of the military for nine months, maybe he was losing his skills.

He'd caught the two bikers off guard, which was how he'd been able to take them both out of action. If there had been more time, he'd have questioned them before rendering them incapacitated. But his only objective was to get Ava out of there.

"I—feel terrible you were forced to kill them because of me." Ava's low voice was full of anguish.

"I didn't kill them." He shot her a sideways glance. "I used only the amount of force necessary to take them out.

They'll have severe headaches when they come to, but they should survive."

"I can understand why you wouldn't want their blood on your hands." Ava stared down at her own hands as if seeing the bloodshed after she'd stabbed the Death Ray.

"I have plenty of blood on my hands," he corrected. "As a Navy SEAL, I shot more men than I care to count to stay alive and execute our missions. They were bad guys, Ava. Terrorists who didn't hesitate to kill innocent people. It's not easy, but I don't lose a whole lot of sleep over what I was forced to do."

She grimaced. "You're just saying that to make me feel better about killing Banjo."

"I'm saying it because it's true. I don't blame you for stabbing Banjo. You did what was necessary to survive." He reached over to take her hand. "I'm proud of you for being so determined to escape Simon and the Death Rays gang. I only wish I could have been there for you sooner."

She gripped his hand tightly, and he wished they weren't driving so he could hold her in his arms. If anyone needed to be held, it was Ava. After a few minutes, she said, "The last guy who tried to help me ended up dead. Brent Green was a decent man who tried to do the right thing. He offered me and Callie protection, and we accepted it. He really liked Callie, and she liked him too. But after he ended up dead in an alley, we both knew we couldn't ask for anyone else's help again."

"How do you know Simon had him killed? Maybe he was the victim of an attempted robbery."

"Because he was stabbed in the neck, the same way I'd stabbed Banjo." She closed her eyes for a long moment. "It was a message for me. One that I haven't forgotten."

"The good news is that I'm better trained." He wasn't

trying to boast about his skills, but he needed her to under-stand where he was coming from. "Nothing bad is going to happen to me, Ava. I can keep you and your baby safe. I hope I proved that back at the motel."

She nodded, but the deep furrow in her brow told him she wasn't convinced.

He drove through the night, heading toward the San Bernardino National Forest. When he reached the casino, he pulled off in a remote corner of the parking lot. Despite the hour being well past two in the morning, there were plenty of vehicles around. He'd suspected as much, casinos could stay open all night if they wanted to.

"Why are we stopping?" Ava asked. She'd continued holding his hand, and he was reluctant to break the physical contact between them.

"I need to check the vehicle for a GPS tracker." He once again raised her hand to his mouth for a reassuring kiss. He managed a smile. "Sit tight with Zulu, this shouldn't take very long."

"Okay." She rested her hands on her belly. He slid out of the driver's seat, then used the flashlight app on his phone to examine the undercarriage.

He found the tracking device near his rear bumper. He plucked the device off his Jeep, then stood and was about to toss it into the woods when he stopped to reconsider. If he did that, Simon's crew would know he'd found it.

He lightly jogged toward the nearest vehicle. He squelched a flash of guilt as he tucked the GPS device beneath the bumper. It was necessary to buy them some time. He sent up a silent prayer for God to keep the owner of the vehicle safe from harm, then turned and hastened back to the Jeep.

"You found something?" Ava's eyes were wide with

surprise. "I don't understand, how did Simon figure out this was your vehicle?"

"Could be he had someone watching the Lizard Lounge, waiting for you to show up." It was the only explanation that made sense to him. He rummaged in the back to find some electrical tape. "Try not to worry. We're truly off-grid now."

"They know your license plate," she protested.

He flashed a grin. "Not for long." He took the electrical tape and went back out to the back of the Jeep. He let Zulu out for a bathroom break as he carefully changed his license plate. What used to be TJ3 A14 became IJ8 AT4. He sat back on his heels, critically surveying his handiwork. It wouldn't hold up under intense scrutiny, but it would be enough to help them stay off Simon's radar.

"Come, Zulu." The Doberman came running at his command, and he took a moment to praise her. Then he opened the back hatch for her to get inside.

He closed Zulu in, then took a glance around the parking lot before heading to the driver's side door. Once they were settled someplace safe, he could take additional precautions. It was too late to get a new vehicle now. He'd have to call one of his Navy SEAL buddies to help him acquire a new one.

Mason and Kaleb were the only two of his teammates still living in California. Mason and Aubrey were in the San Diego area, while Kaleb and Charlotte were outside Los Angeles. The problem was that Mason was married to Aubrey, and they'd recently adopted another child. Kaleb and Charlotte were also pregnant, due at the end of the year. Hudd had settled down in Idaho of all places with his wife, Kendra. Dawson was living in Montana with his wife,

Sylvie, and Dallas was in small-town Texas with his new wife, Maggie.

He hated to bother Mason and Kaleb, especially when they were focused, rightfully so, on their respective families. Yet he knew full well they would drop everything to help him out the moment he asked. As he slid in behind the wheel, he debated whether to head into the San Bernardino National Forest or head back to Los Angeles.

"The Death Rays are headquartered in LA, right?"

"Yes." Ava frowned. "Why?"

As much as he'd rather head into the forest, he turned around in the casino parking lot to head back downtown. "Don't you think that's where he's taken Callie?"

"Probably. Although I think Simon's reach is far and wide, some of the guys he's with are from Mexico." She gently rubbed her belly in a gesture he knew meant to soothe herself and the baby. "I wish I had my phone. I'll never know if I missed Callie's call."

"If she had reached out via phone, I'm sure it was because Simon forced her to." He glanced at her. "LA is a big city with lots of suburbs. I need you to tell me where you think Simon is keeping her."

"It could be anywhere," she said wearily.

He thought about how Simon had killed the man helping her by stabbing him in the neck. "No, I don't think so. I think he has taken Callie right back to where it all started." He paused, then added, "The place from which you escaped."

She sucked in a harsh breath, then slowly nodded. "You're right," she whispered. "I'm sure that's where he's taken Callie. But you need to know that warehouse turned biker pad is in the worst part of the city. It will be dangerous to simply drive in there, much less find a way to get Callie out."

He could easily imagine how Simon had created a safe place for him and his men. He was sure there was other gang activity going on in that area, too, besides just the bikers. But he wasn't about to let that stop him from doing what was necessary. "We'll rescue her, Ava. Have faith."

"What can you do against all of Simon's biker pals?" She glanced at him, her eyes bright with tears. The Ava he knew as a young, somewhat rebellious young woman never cried. He hated knowing that life had beaten her down to the point where she felt so helpless.

"I'll get help from my SEAL buddies. But there will be time to deal with that tomorrow." He wanted her to get the rest she needed. Besides, he wasn't going to head into the middle of a biker gang without a plan. And it would also help to know for sure that's where Callie was before he and the guys went in to rescue her.

He decided to stay in a motel that was on the other side of the city from where they were earlier. He paid for connecting rooms again and asked for a late checkout. The guy behind the desk was willing to cooperate when he set down one hundred dollars on the counter.

The moment Nico had set out to search for Ava, he'd drained his bank accounts so that he would have plenty of cash on hand just for this reason. In the meantime, his retirement checks continued to be deposited from the US government. He could get more if needed, but he still had plenty. Satisfied they were as safe as possible, he hustled Ava and Zulu inside the adjoining rooms.

Ava was still wearing her nightgown, and she shivered in the air-conditioned room. "Have you seen any bugs?"

"No, it looks clean enough." He decided not to mention

the roach traps, similar to what she'd had in her apartment. "Get some rest, Ava."

The moment they'd gotten inside the rooms, she'd used the bathroom. Now she sat on the edge of the bed, twisting her fingers together. "I'm not sure I'll be able to sleep."

"I'll stay with you for a bit." He gestured for her to move over on the bed. She slid beneath the covers as he sat beside her, his back resting on the headboard. "I won't let anything happen to you."

"I know." A ghost of a smile tugged at the corner of her mouth, but then it quickly vanished. It struck him that he had yet to see Ava's full, beautiful smile. It troubled him to know what she'd suffered. Yet he could also admit she was holding up better than he'd expected. Especially considering her pregnancy.

Zulu stretched out on the floor beside the bed. His K9 partner looked up at him for a moment before resting her head between her front paws.

The dog had saved their lives back at the previous motel. He hadn't taken the time to praise her as much as he normally would. Zulu had been his constant companion while recuperating from his ruptured Achilles tendon surgery and over these last months of searching for Ava.

He glanced from Zulu to Ava. She was lying on her side facing him, her hands folded beneath her pillow. Her breathing slowed, and her facial features relaxed as she drifted off to sleep.

She was so beautiful his chest ached. Nico continued watching her, unable to tear his gaze away as he desperately longed for something he couldn't have.

Ava was Jaydon's younger sister. Soon to be a mother. He'd support her in any way he could, but he knew she'd never want the one thing he longed to give her.

His love.

---

AVA SNUGGLED NEXT to the warmth before abruptly jerking awake. Nico? She blinked, then blushed when she realized he'd fallen asleep sitting up against the headboard. Well, sort of sitting up, his body had slid down a bit, his head dangling off at an angle that would no doubt give him a terrible crick in his neck when he awoke.

She watched him for a moment, but all too soon the baby was dancing on her bladder, making it urgent she get up. Carefully, she lifted the sheet and blanket from the other side of the bed and tried to ease away.

"Ava?" Nico's husky voice made her heart thump erratically against her sternum. "Oh, I'm so sorry." The sleepiness in his tone vanished as he practically leaped off the bed as if zapped with a cattle prod. Then Zulu scrambled up too.

"You don't have to apologize." She pushed her curls away from her face as she slid off the bed. Tugging the hem of her nightgown down, she avoided his direct gaze. "I slept the best I have in a long time."

"Oh, ah, good. Glad to hear it." Nico cleared his throat, dragging his hand through his black hair. He told her once his mother was Hispanic, and she could see he'd inherited his mother's bronze skin and dark eyes.

She'd always found him strikingly handsome. So much so that the passing years hadn't lessened her awareness of him one bit.

Inappropriate thing to notice at a time like this. She really needed to pull herself together. "Excuse me." She quickly disappeared into the bathroom.

"Come, Zulu." It was easy to hear Nico talking to Zulu

through the flimsy door. She breathed a sigh of relief that he'd taken Zulu outside, giving her just enough time to use the facilities and to quickly change out of her nightgown.

She chose another sundress to wear, this one bright green. Once it would have accented her auburn-colored hair, but she'd ditched that color a long time ago.

Not that shortening, curling, and dyeing her hair had helped alter her appearance as much as she'd hoped. Simon had still found her.

Her shoulders slumped as she realized he'd never stop looking for her. Never stop hurting those closest to her to get what he wanted.

Revenge.

Banjo had been Simon's second-in-command. They'd been close, as much as dangerous men could be. It was why Simon wanted her dead now too.

When she was ready, she crossed to the connecting door and poked her head through. Zulu was sitting in front of the bathroom door, an empty food and water dish beside her. When she heard the shower going, Ava quickly withdrew to her own room.

She placed her hands over her burning cheeks. Honestly, she needed to get a grip. Nico had rescued her out of loyalty to Jaydon.

Period. End of story.

She took a moment to pack her things in her backpack in case they needed to leave again in a hurry. Just thinking of what the day might hold was enough to make her stomach churn. She knew Nico would want her to take him into Los Angeles, specifically to the warehouse Simon used as a hangout.

The last place on earth she wanted to go.

She drew a deep breath and let it out slowly. She'd do it for Callie.

Her stomach rumbled with hunger. She took a prenatal vitamin out of her backpack but didn't take it. Trial and error had taught her not to take the large vitamins on an empty stomach. Those early months when she'd thrown up first thing every morning had been bad enough. It was only once she'd started taking them with food that she'd felt better.

Nico appeared in the doorway, his dark hair damp from his recent shower. "Are you ready to grab breakfast?" His face creased in a broad smile. "Or should I say brunch? It's almost noon, but I'm sure we can find a place that's still serving breakfast."

"I'm hungry, and so is the baby. I'd love breakfast."

"I have some calls to make, but we should eat first." He headed for the door. "Stay back until I clear the area."

She hovered behind him. It didn't take him long to deem the parking lot and surrounding space safe. "Let's go."

Once they were settled in the Jeep, she said, "I have some money, thankfully my job at the Lizard Lounge provided decent tips."

"No need." There was a hint of steel beneath his tone. "I'll take care of it."

Nico found a family restaurant about two miles away. He pulled into the parking lot, then turned to back into a spot. "Did you see the sign? They serve breakfast all day. I know breakfast used to be your favorite meal."

"It still is," she agreed, surprised he'd remembered. Jaydon used to tease her about it, saying she'd eat breakfast all day if she could. "Thank you."

"My pleasure." He hopped out, then ran around to

open her door. He helped her out, then released the back for Zulu.

"You think they'll let her inside?" She looked at Zulu with doubt. Nico put her on leash, but still the dog looked ferocious. Maybe it was her sharp teeth. "If you ask me, Zulu will scare the customers right out of there."

"They will." He sounded confident as they headed to the door.

"How can you be so sure?" She nodded in thanks when he opened the door for her.

"I've eaten here before." He rested the palm of his hand on her lower back. She wondered if all pregnant women had this weird rush of awareness around handsome men or if it was just her.

"Table for two." When he smiled at the hostess, she beamed back as if Ava wasn't standing right there beside him.

Some men, like Nico Ramirez, were too attractive for their own good. The young woman grabbed two menus. "Of course, this way."

Once they were seated, another server brought water and held up the coffeepot. "Coffee?"

"Yes, please," Nico said.

"Decaf for me." She tried not to sigh. Giving up coffee had been difficult, especially since fatigue was such a big part of being pregnant.

"Caffeine is bad for the baby?" Nico asked with a frown.

"Who knows?" She rolled her eyes. "The first doctor I saw told me one cup of coffee or tea a day was fine, but the next doctor I went to advised me to stop drinking it all together." She waved a hand as the server put a cup in front of her and filled it from a pot with an orange handle. "I'm compromising on one cup of decaf a day."

"Two different doctors?" He looked confused. "I thought most women had one doctor they saw throughout their pregnancy?"

She took a sip of the coffee, eyeing him over the rim. "I've been moving around, so that hasn't been possible."

He frowned. "That's not good, you need consistency. We'll find you a doctor you can stick with throughout the rest of your pregnancy."

She arched a brow. "And how do you propose to do that? I don't have health insurance, so it's not like I have many options. I've gotten pretty good at searching out free health clinics when I'm able. I was supposed to have an appointment in San Bernardino next week, but I don't think that will happen."

He stared at her for a long moment. Before he could say anything, their server returned to take their order. When that was finished, Nico propped his elbows on the table.

She was sitting beside him rather than across, so he turned in his seat to face her. "Ava, I'd like to call my Navy SEAL teammates for help. They care about you because you're Jaydon's sister. They'll want to help find Callie too."

Her stomach tightened with fear. "I don't know if that's a good idea."

"For now, I'm going to ask them to get me a new vehicle, but you have to realize there's no way I can get Callie away from Simon without help." He held her gaze. "You mentioned not wanting me to call law enforcement, but I know a guy who also spent time as a Navy SEAL, and he's a current Los Angeles K9 cop. I'm sure he knows something about the Desert Death Rays motorcycle gang. I'd like to talk to him because the more information I have about them and how they operate, the better."

He was right, and she knew it. If not for Callie falling into Simon's hands, she'd beg Nico to take her to Mexico. She hadn't liked the idea of delivering her baby in a foreign country, especially when she wasn't fluent in the language, but now? She'd gladly take escaping Simon for good over that fear.

Yet she couldn't do it. She couldn't just save herself while leaving Callie to suffer at Simon's hands.

She hated thinking about how much Callie may have suffered already.

"You can call your cop friend to ask about the Desert Death Rays but don't mention me." She lifted her chin stubbornly. "I know you think I won't get in trouble for what I've done, but I'm not willing to take the risk. I will not have my baby in jail. She'll end up in foster care, and who knows when I'd be able to get her back?"

After a long moment, Nico nodded. "I'll keep you out of the conversation. And for now, I'll just ask for help from Mason to get a replacement vehicle since the Jeep was compromised." He leaned forward and lowered his voice. "But soon, Ava, I'll need all my teammates to come here. I can't infiltrate a motorcycle gang without help. And my SEAL teammates are the best at what we do."

"I'm scared, Nico. I don't want you or any of Jaydon's teammates to get hurt because of me. Those men are dangerous. I wouldn't have gotten away if I hadn't caught Banjo off guard. He never considered me a threat."

A hint of a smile tugged at the corner of his mouth. "I told you before, I'm impressed with you, Ava. I give you a lot of credit for escaping them. But I also need you to understand that my teammates have infiltrated terrorist caves in

Afghanistan. We might be older, slightly handicapped, and a bit rusty, but I think we can handle Simon and his goons."

"Handicapped?" She frowned, remembering how he'd come to Jaydon's funeral with his leg in a hard brace after surgery. "Your injury is healed, isn't it?"

"Mostly, yes." He hesitated, then added, "We all carry souvenirs from that last op. But we haven't let our various injuries stop us either. Don't worry, I'm confident we'll find and rescue Callie."

Somehow, she believed him. She wanted to hear more about what the team had suffered, but their server brought their meals. Her stomach rumbled as the scent of eggs and toast reached her.

"Thank you," Nico said. Once the server left, he reached over to take her hand, then bowed his head. "Lord, we ask You to bless this food we are about to eat. We also ask You to continue to keep us safe in Your care. Amen."

"Amen," she echoed softly, humbled by his prayer. Their fingers clung for a moment, his strong hand gently cradling hers. Then he released her.

She pulled out her prenatal vitamin. She tossed it back with a sip of water, then took a bite of her toast. When she was sure she wouldn't throw up, she dug in to her breakfast. Nico's prayer was sweet, but she knew her situation was entirely her own fault. She'd been so stupid, so naïve to go off with Simon willingly.

Now she was pregnant, alone, and scared to death.

No, she wasn't alone anymore. Nico and Zulu were wonderful protectors. This was the safest she had felt in months.

"Everything okay?" Nico asked.

"Fine." She drummed up a weak smile. "Just wishing this peaceful feeling would last a little while."

"It will. I'm just going to gather some information. When we're finished here, we'll head into LA."

Her smile faded. LA held painful memories, but she told herself to get over it. Nothing mattered except saving Callie.

Jayne kicked hard, making her cry out softly. "Oh, wow. That was a strong one."

Nico's eyes widened in horror. "A strong what? Contraction? You're not in labor, are you?"

"No, a kick." She impulsively reached for his hand and placed it on her belly. "This little girl is going to be quite the soccer player."

Nico's hand radiated warmth, and it was only a moment before Jayne kicked again. Nico drew in a quick breath. "That's amazing."

"Yeah, until I'm trying to sleep." She held his hand there for several more beats before releasing him.

"That was incredible, Ava." Nico's husky voice sent a tingle of awareness down her spine. "Thank you for sharing that with me."

"You're welcome." She strove for a light tone, but the stupid hormones caused tears to prick her eyes. She tried to subtly wipe them away but knew Nico's keen gaze noticed her tears.

She continued eating to avoid telling him why she was feeling so emotional. That she wished more than anything that Nico was her baby's father.

## CHAPTER FIVE

The miracle of life shifted and moved beneath his fingertips. Awestruck, Nico had never been so humbled in his life. Men might be physically strong, but only a woman could bring forth a new life.

And that was truly incredible.

"I—thank you for sharing." He could barely think straight. After a few moments, he pulled himself together and looked for their server. Upon catching her eye, he gestured for the check. "We should get out of here."

"And go where?" Ava cradled her mug in her hands. She'd nursed her one cup of decaf throughout their meal. It had to be cold by now.

"I have phone calls to make, and I'll need to let Zulu out soon too." He offered a reassuring smile. "At this point, I'm just doing some intel gathering. Nothing to worry about."

She nodded, but her expression remained full of concern. It bothered him that Ava had been through so much stress during her pregnancy. And without regular medical care either. He needed to find Simon, rescue

Callie, and then figure out a plan to provide for Ava and her baby.

He didn't want to scare her, but there was no way he'd simply walk away once the danger was over. In fact, he'd almost asked her to marry him, specifically for the health care benefits, but had managed to bite his tongue in the nick of time.

His health care benefits were through the VA, but he wasn't sure that would include the cost of giving birth. Kaleb may know more now that his wife was expecting, so he'd have to grill his buddy for information. Even if he had proposed, there was no guarantee Ava would have agreed.

Either way, that would have to wait. He couldn't make plans for the future without dealing with the present threat.

After paying their bill, Nico led Zulu and Ava from the restaurant. There was a cool breeze this morning, unusual for this time of the year. Zulu had her nose up, taking in the interesting scents. He'd done some scent tracking with her in between his various trips to follow leads on Ava, but she was more of a guard dog than anything.

Glancing at Ava now, he silently thanked God again for showing him the path to find her. His job wasn't over, but he was confident he'd be able to mobilize the team once he had verification Callie was being held at Simon's warehouse.

After helping Ava inside, he opened the rear hatch for Zulu. What he needed was a safe place that would allow Zulu some room to run while he made his calls.

"Where are we going?" Ava asked.

"San Bernardino County Regional Park." He glanced at her. "I drove past it on the way in, looks beautiful. Have you been there?"

"No." She shrugged. "Callie and I didn't have a car, so our travel has been limited."

"Well, I think you'll like it." He tried to sound upbeat when inwardly he was deeply troubled by what she had been through. "There's a lake."

"Sounds nice." Her tone was slightly wistful.

As he headed toward the park, he watched the rearview mirror to make sure they weren't followed. It wasn't likely based on the way he'd altered his license plate, but he wasn't going to underestimate Simon's biker thugs again. Which reminded him of a question he'd been meaning to ask. "Ava, did you see Simon break any laws during the time you were with him?"

She slowly shook her head. "I didn't witness any, but I know they were stealing money, and I believe he also killed a couple of guys. He bragged about how scared his men were of him and his getting what he called easy cash. I didn't ask for details, and he didn't offer any." She glanced at him, her expression grave. "I know drugs are involved too, but again, he didn't do those things in front of me. Or if he did, I was clueless." She grimaced. "I was foolishly naïve in those early days we were together."

"It's not your fault, Ava." He was secretly impressed with how she'd taken responsibility for her actions. "How could you know the guy you dated would turn out to be the head of a biker gang?"

"I should have known something was wrong," she insisted. "Looking back, there were plenty of signs I ignored. It pains me to know I was an idiot, but I also can't go back and change the past." She paused, smoothed her hands over her belly, and added, "And despite everything, I don't regret carrying this child."

"Your baby is a blessing, Ava." He tried not to control

the flash of anger over what Simon had done to her. "I know you'll be an amazing mother."

"You do, huh?" She sounded skeptical. "I hope you're right."

"I am." He reached over to take her hand. "And you don't have to handle this alone. I'll be there with you every step of the way."

"That's very sweet, but my child isn't your responsibility." She glanced out her window, then straightened. "Oh, is that the park? It's beautiful."

"Yes, that's it." This was the second time she'd changed the subject when he'd tried to offer his support. Her rejection stung, but he reminded himself that she'd been hiding and on the run for months. It would take time before she'd be able to relax enough to think of something besides basic survival.

At least, he hoped she would. Nico could accept she wasn't interested in him romantically, but surely she'd accept his support and friendship.

He parked the Jeep, then gestured toward a cluster of picnic tables. "We'll head over there, okay?"

"It's more than okay. It's perfect." She smiled, the first real smile that brightened her blue eyes.

He decided to leave Zulu off leash. The poor dog had been cooped up for longer than usual these past few days, and when he tossed the tennis ball and yelled, "Fetch," she ran after it, her speed and agility impressive.

"She's fast."

"Yep." He tossed the ball several more times as Ava sat at the picnic table watching with admiration. Then he pulled out his phone. The first call he made was to his buddy Bryce Flynn.

"Flynn," Bryce answered in a professional tone.

"Bry, it's Nico. I need some info, do you have a minute?"

"Uh, yeah. Hold on." There were muffled sounds in the background before Bryce said, "Okay, I'm outside the office taking Kirby on a break. What's going on?"

"What do you know about Simon Marks, a.k.a. Simon Normandy, and the Desert Death Rays motorcycle gang?" Nico knew Bryce had a male German shepherd named Kirby as his K9 partner.

"I'm not familiar with Simon, but the gang squad is watching the Death Rays," Bryce admitted. "Why do you ask?"

"Why are they on your radar?"

Bryce hesitated, then said, "Because we have reason to believe they're dangerous. Not just in dealing drugs but in armed robbery along with assault and battery. Come on, Nico, what are you not telling me?"

He knew Ava was listening to his side of the conversation, so he chose his words carefully. "I have reason to believe they recently kidnapped a woman at gunpoint from a restaurant in San Bernardino."

"Do you have proof?" Bryce sounded excited. "We'd love to nail them for something, so far everything we've tried to pin on them hasn't stuck. They have a way of eliminating witnesses too."

That wasn't reassuring, but Nico knew he shouldn't have expected anything less. "Does the LAPD have anyone on the inside?"

"I can't answer that, Nico, I'm not part of the gang unit." Bryce sounded irritated. "Why don't you come talk to me in person? If you have evidence of a kidnapping done at the hands of the Death Rays, I'd love to see it."

"I might have something for you," Nico said. Ava shook

her head no, but he continued. "I'll see what I can do. I needed to know if you had anything else on them that might help get this woman back."

"Lots of suspicion without any proof," Bryce said. "But you're not a cop, Nico. You need to stay away from the Death Rays, understand?"

"I hear you, Bryce. Thanks for taking the time to talk to me. I'll check in with you later," he promised before ending the call.

"Thank you for not mentioning me, but I don't think Callie wants the police involved either," Ava said. "We both agreed to stay far away from the cops."

"I didn't give him anything." At least not yet. But Nico did plan to share the Lizard Lounge video with Bryce very soon. He held up his phone and called Mason Gray. His SEAL buddy didn't answer, so he left a brief message. "Yo, Senior Chief. It's Nico. I need a favor. Call me back, thanks."

"Senior Chief?" Ava echoed. "Is Mason your boss?"

"Not anymore," Nico said with a grin. "Mason was the highest-ranking member of our team and took the lead on our various ops. We're all retired now, though. Honorably and medically discharged from service."

"Sounds like you guys were very close." Grief filled her eyes.

"Jaydon had a lot of respect for Mason, like the rest of us did." He tossed the ball again for Zulu, then crossed over to sit beside her. "I'm sorry about Jaydon. We did everything we could, including performing CPR while we were still in the water. I desperately wish we could have saved him."

"Jay accepted the risks of being a SEAL." She managed

a sad smile. "He loved you guys as much if not more than his family."

"Not more than you, Ava," Nico corrected. "He adored you."

"There were eight years between us," she murmured. "I was ten when he joined the Navy. But even though I only saw him when he was on leave, I looked up to him. I was proud of what he accomplished. And I still miss him."

Jaydon had been his swim buddy, and losing him had been akin to losing a limb. Nico still looked for Jaydon, expecting him to be nearby even though he knew his long-time friend was gone. "I know, Ava. I miss him too."

His phone rang, Mason's name flashing on the screen. "Thanks for calling me back."

"Do you have good news?" Mason asked. "A lead on Ava?"

"Yes, I found her. She's safe, Mason."

"Praise the Lord," Mason said in relief. "That's the best news I've heard all year."

"It's wonderful news," Nico agreed. He ignored Ava's frown and added, "But she's not out of danger yet, which is why I need a favor. My Jeep is compromised, I need a new ride, one that will accommodate Zulu."

"Done. Where are you? I'll arrange for a rental under my name."

"I'm in San Bernardino, but we can travel to Riverside." The city wasn't exactly on the way back to Los Angeles but close enough. "I'd rather pick up something there."

"Can do," Mason agreed. "Give me an hour to make the arrangements, I'll shoot you a text when I'm finished."

"Thanks. That's a huge help."

"Anytime." Mason waved away his gratitude. "Nico?"

"Yeah?"

"Are you sure Ava is all right?"

Now wasn't the time to explain about her pregnancy. "She's fine, but a friend of hers is in danger. I may need backup soon, but I know you've recently added to your family, and Kaleb's wife is expecting too."

"You say the word, and we'll be there," Mason said firmly. "All of us will drop what we're doing to help. You're not alone in this, Nico."

"Thanks. I'll probably take you up on that offer." He was grateful to have friends like Mason, Kaleb, Hudd, Dawson, and Dallas. "Stay close to your phones. Oh, and do me a favor, call the rest of the guys to let them know I've found Ava. I know they'll be glad to hear the news."

"They will, we've all been praying for her safe return," Mason assured him. "Call anytime, Nico. I'll be there as soon as possible."

"Thanks again for that and the rental car. Talk to you later." He ended the call, noticing Ava regarding him curiously. "Every guy on our SEAL team will be thrilled to hear you're alive and well, Ava."

She flushed and glanced at her belly. "They'll think less of me once they realize what I've done. Especially since they're Christians."

"No, they won't think less of you. I promise, they won't judge. We've all made mistakes." He stepped closer. "My friend Dallas? He went back home to discover he had an eight-year-old daughter he'd never known about. And now he's recently married his daughter's mother."

"Really?" Her gaze looked wistful for a moment, as if that news had eased her concerns. "Okay, what next?"

"After we pick up our rental in Riverside, we'll need to head into Los Angeles." He winced when the light faded from her eyes. "You don't have to take me all the way to

Simon's hangout, but if you could draw me a map, that would help."

"I'll take you." She sounded resigned. "But I don't think you should go into the warehouse alone. Simon has added more men to his gang."

"I won't. But I need to know what I'm dealing with before I call in the others to help." He didn't add that they'd need time to assemble some weapons and other devices to use to infiltrate the warehouse safely.

He didn't want Ava to worry any more than she already was. He'd agreed to find and free Callie, but his main goal was still Ava's safety.

She wouldn't like it, but he planned to enlist Bryce Flynn's help to protect her while he and the rest of his team went in to rescue Callie.

Ava and her unborn child needed to be protected at all costs. No matter what.

---

THE BEAUTIFUL SERENITY of the San Bernardino County Regional Park was a nice reprieve from the mess she'd made of her life.

No, she refused to think of Jayne as a problem. But Callie's being taken by Simon certainly was.

Listening to Nico talking to his SEAL team leader had filled her with fear. She knew he was planning to invade Simon's warehouse to rescue Callie.

If Callie was there. Her stomach tightened with concern for her friend. She abruptly reached for Nico's hand. "Will you pray for Callie? Her last name is Burgess."

"Of course." He bowed his head. "Lord, we know You care about Your children. Please keep Callie Burgess safe in

Your care until we can find and free her from the terrible men who have taken her. Amen."

"Amen," she whispered. Oddly, a sense of peace washed over her, along with a flash of hope. "Thank you. That was very nice."

"God is here for you too, Ava." He smiled and stood, helping her to her feet. "After all, God showed me the way here to find you."

Truthfully, her meltdown that had led her to call her friend Jill had been the reason he'd found her, but maybe that was God's plan. What did she know? She hadn't continued going to church after she'd moved out of her parents' house. Especially after they'd been killed in a car crash. Why God had taken them was a mystery. Jaydon had tried to comfort her, to explain that it wasn't up to them to question God's plan, but she hadn't bought into his theory.

Now, standing beside Nico in the beautiful park with Zulu sitting beside them, she couldn't help but wonder if Jaydon had been right. That she was only here right now with Nico because of God's plan.

Nico had called her baby a blessing, and she knew that much was true. She'd made terrible decisions, but for the first time in months, she had hope for the future.

"We need to go. I'm sure traffic will be a nightmare," Nico murmured.

"Maybe not so bad to Riverside, but LA? Yeah, that has only gotten worse over the years." She forced a smile and began walking toward the Jeep. "I've never been to Riverside, what's it like?"

"I've only been there once. It's a quaint city." He helped her into the passenger seat before taking Zulu around back.

They listened to the radio as they drove toward Riverside. Ava found herself relaxing and enjoying this time with

Nico. If she had her way, they'd head straight to the border, leaving Simon and the Desert Death Rays behind.

But she couldn't do that to Callie. Leaving her friend behind was not an option. All she could do was hope and pray the younger woman was still alive.

The ride to Riverside took roughly thirty minutes. She wasn't surprised to learn the rental car Mason had secured was waiting for them when they arrived. She slid out of the passenger seat, then reached for her backpack.

"I'll get that," Nico said, quickly taking the pack.

"I'm not helpless," she protested.

Nico ignored her comment and went to work, quickly moving all their belongings, including supplies for Zulu, to the new SUV that was larger than his Jeep.

"All set?" He glanced at her expectantly.

"Yes." She swallowed a lump of fear. "Let's head into Los Angeles."

That drive took longer, not because of the distance but because of the overall insane traffic. They were bumper-to-bumper well before they hit the city limits.

She gave Nico directions, her stomach tightening with every passing mile. Finally, she gripped his arm. "See that exit up ahead? That's the one that will lead to Simon's place."

"Does Simon's place have a name?" Nico asked.

She let out a choked laugh. "Stanley's Shoes, although the lettering on the outside of the building has faded over time. Based on the number of motorcycles that will be parked out front, no one would mistake it for a shoe warehouse."

"Are there other buildings nearby?"

She thought about his question for a long moment. It had been February that she'd escaped, and much of that night, other than stabbing Banjo in the neck, was a blur. "There is another warehouse right next door, which may belong to Simon now too."

"Okay." He didn't seem overly concerned with her lack of detail. "We won't get too close, but I need a spot where I can use binoculars to check the place out."

Her stomach tightened further. "I'm sorry, but I don't know of a place for you to do that. Maybe we should turn around and go back to San Bernardino."

"Have faith in me, Ava. I won't put you in harm's way." He smiled gently, then took the exit. He found a place to pull over, then reached for his phone. "I'll find something nearby."

"You think Stanley's Shoes will show up after all these years?" She scoffed. "Not likely."

"You'd be surprised. Look. Here's what the place used to look like, and there's an address too." He grinned. "Piece of cake."

Maybe she had underestimated his abilities. She'd been off-grid for so long she'd forgotten what a smartphone could do. She drew in a deep breath and nodded. Nico was a man of faith, surely God would protect him. "I'm glad."

He surprised her by leaning over to give her a sisterly kiss on the cheek. The sweet caress was over before she realized what was happening, and she had to stop herself from lifting her hand to touch the spot. Nico didn't seem to notice her reaction as he shifted the SUV into gear and pulled out onto the road. "There's a hill with residential houses on it not far from the warehouse. We'll check that out first."

A residential neighborhood sounded like a good place to go, although this location of the city was known to be dangerous.

Not as dangerous as Simon's warehouse but not safe either.

"You know those are probably low-income housing projects," she said as he turned at the next intersection.

"I'm armed. And we have Zulu too." He shot her a sideways glance. "Try not to worry, it's not good for the baby."

"I know." She'd been working on reducing her stress for a long time now, ever since she'd realized she was pregnant. Yet, being this close to Simon's warehouse made it difficult to maintain her composure.

He was like the boogeyman, larger than life in her mind. And twice as dangerous.

Nico pulled over again a short time later. "Here, you drive for a bit."

"Me?" She didn't move. "You know I haven't driven a car for about a year now, right?"

"It's like riding a bike." He flashed another of his handsome grins. "You'll be fine. I need to scope things out."

They switched seats. She pulled the seat forward until she could reach the pedals, which only left a gap of slightly more than an inch between her belly and the steering wheel. Apparently, her driving days were numbered.

It took a few minutes for her to become familiar with the vehicle. The brakes seemed unusually touchy, but Nico didn't say anything about her abrupt stops. He had the binoculars up to his eyes, scanning the area outside the passenger-side window.

"Found it," he finally said. "See if you can find a parking spot nearby."

Parking in LA was laughable, but she did her best. She memorized the street names so she didn't veer too far off course from where he'd spotted the warehouse. She was on her second pass when she glanced in the rearview mirror. A man wearing jeans low on his hips, a baseball cap backward on his head, slid behind the wheel of a rusty Buick. Seconds later, he pulled the vehicle away from the curb.

She hit the brake, giving Nico a jolt. Thankfully, Zulu was lying down or she thought the poor dog would have been knocked off balance too.

Nico turned and arched a brow. "You okay?"

"I told you I was rusty." She felt like an idiot but put the car in reverse so she could swoop in to grab the parking spot. She wanted to let Nico take over to parallel park, something she hadn't done in well over a year, but gritted her teeth and forced herself to remember the procedure.

It took her three tries, but she finally got the angle right to park. When she finished, she sat back with a sigh. "I did it."

"You sure did. Nice job." He didn't tease her about her pathetic parking attempts, just pushed open the car door.

"Wait! Where are you going?" She grabbed his arm.

"I'm just going to step out to see if I can visualize the warehouse." He patted her hand. "I won't leave you."

She knew he meant that as a temporary thing. Soon he would leave her to rescue Callie. She let go and watched as he stood on the running board of the SUV and raised the binoculars to his eyes.

"That's definitely the place," he muttered. Lowering the binoculars, he stepped down. "Ava? I need you to take a look."

"Me?" Her voice came out high and squeaky, but she slid out from behind the wheel and joined him. She stepped up on the running board and leaned on the open door. Nico stood beside her, supporting her too.

"I want you to tell me if you see Simon."

Swallowing against the lump of fear in her throat, she

took the binoculars and looked in the direction where she estimated the warehouse to be. It took her a few minutes to figure out how to work the lenses so she could see clearly. From there, she moved the binoculars slowly from one biker to the next.

Then she found him. Simon with his long hair pulled back from his head, wearing a black leather skullcap and matching black leather vest. He stood with a cigarette dangling from the corner of his mouth.

Beads of sweat popped out along her skin as she saw for the first time in months the man of her worst nightmares.

# CHAPTER SIX

When Ava's body began to tremble, Nico tightened his grip around her, then reached up to take the binoculars. She released them and leaned against him as if her strength was waning. He'd known bringing Ava back here would be difficult for her. And if he could have spared her the angst, he would have. "Easy, he can't hurt you." He lifted the binoculars. "Tell me which guy is Simon."

"He's thinner than most of them." Her voice was tense as if just seeing him had ratcheted her stress level up several notches. "His long, dark hair is pulled back, and he's wearing a skullcap on his head. He's smoking and has a scar along the side of his cheek."

"I see him." He quickly imprinted Simon's facial features on his memory. The distance was too far to get a decent picture with his cell phone, he'd need a telescopic camera for that. Something to think about to share a picture of the guy with the rest of his team. He took another long moment to search for the dark-haired Callie, but he didn't see any women outside the warehouse.

He frowned, finding that curious. Most motorcycle

clubs had plenty of women members. Tough women that could hold their own within the gang.

"Hey, what are you doing?" A sharp voice had him lowering the binoculars and turning. Three Hispanic men stood on the other side of the rental SUV, their arms crossed over their chests as they stared at him defiantly. The leader was the guy in the middle, he was maybe a step ahead of the other two. "You don't belong here."

"Says who?" Nico subtly moved so that Ava could slide into the passenger seat. Then he dug out the key fob and released the back hatch. A growling Zulu leaped down, baring her teeth at the strangers.

Instantly, the group of three moved back. Nico closed the door to protect Ava, then pulled his weapon as he came around the front of the car. "We're leaving, but you three need to back off." He gestured with his gun. "Before someone gets hurt."

He didn't doubt the men were armed, but thankfully, they didn't reach for their guns. If they had, he'd have shot them. The group of three took another step back and then another. Zulu continued to bark and growl, and it was only once the guys were well outside of range that he said, "Get in, Zulu."

The dog wheeled and jumped into the back hatch. Using the key fob, he closed the hatch, then slid in behind the wheel and started the engine. He held the gun in his hand as he pulled out of the parking space. He was keenly aware of the three men watching from a distance as he drove away.

"I told you it wasn't a good area," Ava said, her voice shaky. "You know they probably had guns."

"I know they did, but I also suspected they weren't ready to get in a full-fledged gunfight either." He glanced at her and tucked the Sig Sauer beneath his leg. "And I needed to see the layout of the area around the warehouse."

"Well, you found it," she said on a sigh. He noticed she was doing that smoothing-her-hands-over-her-belly thing and sensed she was trying to lower her stress level.

"Yes, but there was no sign of Callie." He frowned. "And no other women milling about either. That seems odd to me."

"There are some women who are there voluntarily, but not many." She grimaced. "The guys tend to take women against their will, forcing them into submission. But there are a few who don't mind being a part of the gang, eagerly participating in breaking the law."

He wished he had a way to bring Simon down, but he had to remain focused on the main issue of rescuing Callie. He hated adding to her stress level, but he asked, "Do you think you could draw me a map of the warehouse interior? I need specifics around where you believe Callie is likely being held."

"Yes, that's fine." She grimaced and shifted in her seat. "Where are we going?"

"I'll find a motel." He didn't like the way she looked. "Are you feeling okay?"

"I have some nausea." Her voice sounded weak. "I'm sure it's nothing."

He wasn't convinced. She hadn't mentioned feeling ill yesterday. "Have you been feeling sick to your stomach all along?"

"Not really. Mostly just in those early months." She rested her head back against the seat and closed her eyes.

He continued driving, casting glances at her every few minutes. Ava looked pale and clearly didn't feel well. Had seeing Simon again brought this on? Nico swallowed hard, wishing he knew more about pregnancy-related stress. Something he needed to research, especially since Ava hadn't been seen regularly by a doctor.

A situation that needed to change ASAP. He desperately wanted to go watch the warehouse to find Callie before calling in the troops, but that was a task easier done at night. In the meantime, he needed to ensure Ava and her baby got the care they needed. Surely there was a free women's health clinic nearby.

And if not? He'd take her to a regular doctor and pay the bill out of his pocket. Nothing was more important than making sure Ava and the baby were healthy.

Not even finding Callie.

The thought made him wince. Okay, finding an innocent, kidnapped woman was important too. Nico decided to treat this like every other op he and his SEAL teammates had gone on.

Gather intel, make a plan, and move in. The SEAL mantra was that the only easy day was yesterday. Tonight, the minute he verified Callie was being held in the warehouse, he'd call in the rest of his team. He was confident they'd be able to get in and out without difficulty.

"Pull over." Ava's hoarse voice interrupted his thoughts. He quickly did, and seconds later, she'd opened the passenger-side door, bent over, and threw up.

A wave of panic hit hard. He rummaged in the vehicle, but the rental didn't have any spare napkins tucked in the center console. Releasing his seat belt, he reached back for his duffel and pulled out the shirt he'd worn yesterday. "Here, use this."

Ava didn't argue. Taking the shirt, she used it to wipe her face. "I don't understand," she murmured, sitting back against the seat, again with her eyes closed. "I haven't gotten sick like this in months."

"We need to get you in to see a doctor." He tightened his grip on the steering wheel. "I'll find the closest emergency department."

"No need. Just give me a few minutes." She left the car door open as if worried she might upchuck again. Nico hated feeling helpless; it wasn't in his nature to sit and do nothing while someone needed help.

Especially not when that person was the woman he'd secretly cared about and admired for years.

"Ava, you need to see a doctor." It wasn't easy to quell the panic clawing up his back. "I'm sure getting sick like this isn't normal."

"What do you know about a normal pregnancy?" She must be feeling a little better because her usual feistiness had returned. "Okay, I think I'm fine now." She reached over to close the car door. "Let's go."

He wasn't about to be deterred from getting her medical attention. Maybe he didn't know what was normal when it came to being pregnant, but this was her first time too. Using his phone, he pulled up the closest emergency department. Memorizing the location, he headed in that direction.

It wasn't until he got close that Ava lifted her head. "I told you I don't need to go to the ER."

"How do you know that?" He strove to keep his tone easy and nonconfrontational. "You haven't been seen by a doctor in a while, what harm can there be in getting checked out?"

"ER visits cost an arm and a leg," she muttered. "I'm only supposed to go there if I'm in labor, which I'm not. Besides, an urgent clinic would be cheaper."

"I don't care about the cost. I care about you and your baby." He drew in a deep breath and hung on to his temper. He didn't understand her comment about only going to the ER if she was in labor, then realized that might be because she didn't have a regular doctor. The thought made him angry all over again. "Ava, I have plenty of money. Going to the ER means access to an OB doc. Which is what you need, and I doubt that would happen if we chose the urgent care route."

"I feel better," she protested.

"I'm glad. But it's important that we have you examined by a professional." He was tired of arguing with her. Thankfully, the hospital was up ahead. Following the red emergency signs, he found the parking lot.

Leaving Zulu in the car wasn't an option. He squashed a pang of guilt as he rummaged in the back for the dog vest he carried. She wasn't exactly a service dog, but Zulu was well trained and wouldn't cause a problem either.

Once he had Zulu's vest on and clipped to the leash, he went around to help Ava out. She reluctantly accompanied him inside, and he tried not to groan when he realized how crowded the waiting room was.

"Told you this was a bad idea," she said in a low voice. "We'll be here for hours."

"I don't care." He led her to the triage desk.

"Are you in labor?" the woman asked, eyeing Ava curiously.

"No," she answered honestly.

"She just threw up and hasn't been feeling well. I'm concerned there's something serious going on with her or the baby," Nico said firmly. "She hasn't been able to see an obstetrician on a regular basis; it's been well over a month since her last visit."

"Okay, please provide your name and insurance information." If the woman was annoyed at their using the ER for something like a pregnancy checkup, she didn't let on. But she did frown at bit at the dog. She didn't say anything because of the service vest he'd placed over Zulu's body.

"No insurance, but I'll pay for the visit." Nico turned to Ava, indicating she should provide the rest of the information.

Ava used her real name and pulled out her driver's license for identification. It made him wonder how she'd gotten the job at the Lizard Lounge under the name Renee. He assumed Pedro hadn't asked too many questions and likely paid the employees in cash.

Not his problem, he was just glad Pedro had offered Ava and Callie jobs when they'd needed them the most.

The wait didn't take as long as he feared, maybe Ava's being pregnant had helped. After thirty minutes, they were escorted back to a room. Ava sat on the edge of the cot rather than lying down.

"What brings you in today?" the nurse asked, giving Zulu a curious glance as she unraveled a blood pressure cuff and placed it over Ava's upper arm. Since the dog wasn't growling or barking, she didn't protest.

"I haven't been feeling well," Ava admitted. She seemed resigned to go through the visit. "I've experienced some bad headaches recently, and I threw up about an hour ago, the urge came out of the blue."

"Hmm." The nurse placed a stethoscope in her ears and proceeded to check Ava's blood pressure. She frowned, then pulled the earpieces out of her ears. "Ava, I need you to lie down."

"Why?" Nico asked as Ava did as the nurse suggested.

"Her blood pressure is a bit high," the nurse said evasively. "I'll recheck it again in a few minutes."

"That's strange, on my previous visits my blood pressure has always been low," Ava said with a frown.

"You've been under some stress lately," Nico reminded her.

"Rest for a few minutes, I'll be back soon." The nurse left the room, closing the curtain behind her.

Nico knew the nurse was worried, he'd seen it in her eyes. His suspicions were confirmed when the nurse returned five minutes later accompanied by a doctor dressed in scrubs.

"I'm Dr. Abrams," he introduced himself. "I specialize in OB. You mentioned not feeling well?"

"More tired than usual, with some headaches. But today I threw up, which was really strange," Ava said.

"You're how far along?" he asked.

"I'm due mid-November, in about eight weeks."

"I see, so you're thirty-three weeks along. We're going to check a few things to make sure you and your baby are fine, but first I'm going to ask Tina to take your blood pressure again."

The nurse Tina stepped forward to recheck Ava's blood pressure. She did it manually, but as he watched the needle on the dial, Nico noticed it bounce at the 190 mark. Tina took her time, then removed the cuff and turned to Dr. Abrams. "It's still very high."

"How high?" Ava asked.

"One ninety-six over one twelve," Tina replied.

"She may have preeclampsia," Dr. Abrams said. "We'll run some additional tests after I take a listen to the baby."

Nico didn't have any idea what preeclampsia was, but it

didn't sound good. He sank into the closest chair, instinctively knowing Ava wouldn't be discharged anytime soon.

He silently thanked God that he'd overridden Ava's concerns to bring her in. Whatever this preeclampsia was, he knew it was serious.

---

THE WAY the doctor and nurse hovered over her told Ava this was a bigger deal than she'd anticipated. Her blood pressure was sky high, and that was not normal.

Was this the result of something she'd done? Or hadn't done? Like going in for regular prenatal checkups? Guilt shrouded her, making her wish once again she'd managed to get away from Simon without stabbing Banjo.

Yet during the last doctor appointment she'd had, everything had been fine. Her blood pressure, along with her other vital signs, was normal. She'd been assured the baby was growing well and that she'd done well as far as not gaining too much weight, despite the way she could barely see her toes.

As Dr. Abrams listened to her baby's heart rate, she reached out to Nico. He instantly inched his chair closer so he could take her hand. She clung to him, trying to calm her racing heart. Being stressed was likely what had gotten her into this situation. She was equally determined to de-stress her way out of it.

From her angle lying on the bed, she couldn't see the Doberman, but she assumed Zulu was near Nico. One thing was for certain, the medical staff didn't seem at all concerned about the dog.

No, they were singularly focused on her. And her baby.

Preeclampsia? What was that? She didn't want to

believe it was as bad as it sounded. She focused on taking slow, deep, calming breaths. Ava knew she could bring her blood pressure down by focusing on her body. And for the first time in what seemed like forever, she sent up a silent prayer.

*Please, Lord. I know I don't deserve Your grace, but please help save my baby.*

"Baby's heart rate is good, but I think we'll get her hooked up to a fetal monitor just to keep a closer eye on it," Dr. Abram's said. "I'd like a urine sample sent for a protein analysis."

"What is preeclampsia?" Nico asked. She sent him a thankful glance for the question. She continued taking slow, deep breaths to bring down her blood pressure.

"We don't know for sure she has it," Dr. Abrams cautioned. "It's a syndrome that is experienced by roughly six percent of all first-time moms. It primarily occurs with first pregnancies, rarely subsequent ones. I will say that high blood pressure and protein spilling into the urine are key symptoms."

"You think I threw up because my blood pressure was high?" It made sense. She realized now that her headache had spiked mere moments before the urge to get sick overwhelmed her.

Nurse Tina checked her blood pressure again, then glanced at Dr. Abrams. "It's coming down, but still high at one seventy-two over ninety-six."

"Great." Dr. Abrams smiled reassuringly. "Your blood pressure is starting to come down, which is a good thing. And yes, I think your body was reacting to an unusually high blood pressure. Resting already seems to be working."

She nodded and glanced at Nico. After Dr. Abrams and Tina left the room, she said, "You were right to bring me in."

"I'm glad you and the baby seem to be doing better." To his credit, he didn't bring up the way she hadn't wanted to come. "And now we know that a headache and an abrupt onset of nausea is a sign of your blood pressure spiking too high."

"Yes, that makes sense." She kept her voice calm and continued to take slow, relaxing breaths. It seemed to be working. "I'm hoping that once my vital signs return to normal, they'll let me go."

Nico nodded, but then said, "Only if the doctor says you and the baby are stable. Promise me you'll follow the doctor's orders."

"I promise." She brushed off the flash of irritation, it wasn't worth the added stress. "I would never put my baby at risk."

"I know you won't."

"Ms. Rampart?" Tina returned to the room. "Do you think you can provide a urine sample?"

"Yes." She had needed to go to the bathroom for a while now, but she hadn't wanted to bother Nico. Her cheeks flushed with embarrassment, but she told herself to get over it. Nico had been a gentleman, always offering her privacy.

And she'd soon learned that when you were pregnant, privacy went out the window.

"Are you sure it's okay for her to get up and move around?" Nico's tone was laced with concern. "I can carry her."

"No need," Tina assured him. "Resting is good, but she can certainly get up to use the restroom."

The idea of Nico carrying her made her flush deepen. Hadn't he noticed the size of her belly? She was too big to be carried around.

After using the bathroom, she had to smile as Zulu got

up from the floor to wag her backside with excitement at seeing her. "You're a good girl, Zulu." She paused to stroke the Doberman's sleek fur.

"Let me help you." Nico rose and offered his hand. She took it, then surprised herself by giving him a hug.

"Having you here makes all the difference," she said, her voice muffled against his soft T-shirt.

"I'll always be here for you, Ava." He gathered her close, pressing a kiss to the top of her head. She secretly wished he'd kiss her like a woman he wanted, not as the younger sister of his close friend.

"Thank you." She could have stayed nestled in his arms forever, but she forced herself to step away. Pregnancy hormones were dangerous, making her long for something more. Something Nico would never offer.

Oh, he'd said he'd always be there to support her, and she believed him. But she didn't want Nico to be stuck with her out of duty. She knew he would do just about anything for her out of a long-standing loyalty to her dead brother.

Once, Ava had prided herself on being strong. She'd been determined to make her own way in the world. But then she'd made one bad decision after another. Which had resulted in her being in this position.

Letting Nico give up his life for her was not an option. He deserved to find a woman to love and who would love him too.

At this point, she wasn't even sure she was capable of true love. These days, it was difficult to trust her volatile emotions.

"Are you okay?" Nico's concern brought the ridiculous prick of tears to her eyes. See? This was exactly what she was talking about. She didn't recognize this weepy woman she'd turned into.

"Yes, I'm fine." She turned toward the bed, awkwardly sliding up onto the mattress. Nico hovered beside her as if he feared she'd faint from the effort.

"All set?" Tina returned with a smile. She disappeared into the bathroom, then brought out the sample. After a few minutes, Tina returned. "I'm going to double-check your blood pressure again."

Thankfully, her blood pressure was even lower. Ava took that as a good sign. Her deep breathing was having a positive impact.

Another nurse came in to attach a device to her abdomen. "My name is Emily, I work with Dr. Abrams. This is a baby monitor, it will track your baby's heartbeat real time."

"Sounds good." She lifted her hips off the bed so the nurse could place the band around her entire belly. Then she moved the monitor around until the baby's heartbeat showed up on the screen.

"Your baby's pulse is one twenty-two, which is perfectly normal," Emily said with a smile.

"How long will I need to wear this?" Based on the size of the machine, she didn't get the impression it was something portable to take home with her.

"Just for a little while. I'm sure Dr. Abrams will be back soon." Emily watched the tracing on the machine for another moment, then turned to leave.

"It's amazing that we can see the baby's heart rate," Nico said softly.

"Yeah." She turned her head to face him. "I'm growing concerned they're going to make me stay the night."

"Stress isn't good for the baby, so don't worry," Nico said. "Besides, staying here is not the end of the world, Ava. You'll be safe here."

It wasn't her safety she was concerned about. "What about Callie? The longer Simon has her, the more she'll suffer." *Because of me*, she thought but didn't say.

No stress. She took another slow, even breath. *No stress.*

"I plan to find Callie, but I can't sneak up on the place until nighttime." Nico smiled reassuringly. "Leave Callie to me. You just focus on yourself and the baby."

"I'll try." Easier said than done. Although she couldn't deny that having Callie safe would be on large burden off her shoulders.

But Simon would still loom out there as a threat.

"Ms. Rampart?" Dr. Abrams pushed the curtain aside and strode into the room. "How are you feeling?"

"Much better." She caught Nico's arched gaze and added, "I don't have a headache or feel sick to my stomach like I did before. I would tell you if I did."

"Glad to hear it." He took a moment to watch her baby's heart rate, then turned to face her. "Your urine test showed that you have some protein in your urine. Not as much as I'd expected based on how high your blood pressure was, but more than is normal."

"What's normal?" she asked.

"None," he said frankly. "Based on your blood pressure and your urine protein, I'm diagnosing you with a mild form of preeclampsia. As I mentioned, this phenomenon impacts roughly six percent of all women during their first pregnancy. You didn't do anything to cause this," he added. "It's just something that happens. The good news is that I don't think your condition is serious enough that we need to induce labor."

"Wait, what? Induce labor? I still have eight weeks to go!"

"I know, and that's why we'd like you to keep that little

bun of yours cooking in the oven for a while longer." Dr. Abrams smiled gently. "I'd like you to stay overnight, and if things look good in the morning, you can be discharged as long as you rest."

"Define rest," Nico said.

"Stay off your feet except to walk short distances, rest, and generally relax." He smiled kindly. "Every week you can put off having your baby improves the baby's chances of doing well once he or she is born. A baby's lungs develop faster when the mother is under stress from conditions like preeclampsia. The problem would be if the preeclampsia gets worse, to the point it's eclampsia. The biggest fear with eclampsia is having seizures, and that could cause a fetal demise. I'm not trying to scare you," he hastened to reassure her, no doubt seeing the stark fear in her eyes. "You're not at that point yet. Far from it. Our goal, of course, is to keep it that way."

Ava glanced at Nico, who stood and took her hand. "Of course, we'll do whatever you say, doc."

She nodded in agreement, although her thoughts were whirling. Dr. Abrams made it sound like she was having this baby sooner rather than later. A possibility she'd never considered.

*Dear Lord, keep my baby safe in Your loving care!*

# CHAPTER SEVEN

Preeclampsia. As if Callie being taken at gunpoint wasn't bad enough, now Nico had to worry about Ava and the possibility of delivering a premature baby.

The doc seemed reassured she was doing better, which helped. And if he were honest, Nico would admit that having Ava here at the hospital was the perfect way to keep her safe while he went to case the Desert Death Rays' warehouse. Once he'd confirmed Callie was in there and alive, he'd call the rest of his SEAL teammates so they could come up with a plan of attack to get her out.

And to take care of Simon once and for all.

Not that he planned to kill the guy outright. But he was sure they could find something inside the warehouse to use against him, drugs or illegal guns. He made a mental note to call his law enforcement buddy Bryce to let him know their plan. He'd keep Ava's secret for as long as possible.

Very soon all Ava would need to worry about was resting for the next several weeks until it was time for her to have her baby.

The way it should be.

"Do you think he's right about the fact that I didn't cause this?" Ava asked.

"Yes, he wouldn't lie to you." He reached out to take her hand. "It sounds like preeclampsia is just one of those things that happens to some pregnant mothers. Being under stress didn't cause it, but the cure is to rest and relax. I'm glad they're keeping you here overnight."

"It's better to be safe, isn't it?" She glanced over to where the baby's heart rate pulsed on the screen. "I never imagined I'd have this baby early. I heard women tended to go a week late in their first pregnancy."

Nico doubted she'd make it to her due date, but he wasn't going to tell her his fears. "The doc said you're doing better. Look how well your blood pressure came down? Just concentrate on getting lots of rest."

She nodded. "That seems to be working."

Thankfully, she wasn't working at the Lizard Lounge anymore. All those hours standing on her feet would not be considered restful.

Nico was anxious to find Callie and get Simon taken care of so that he could focus on Ava and her baby.

Tina came into the room. "Ms. Rampart? We're transferring you to a room in the OB unit."

"Okay." Ava appeared subdued. "Thank you."

"They found a room at the end of a hall so you won't be disturbed by crying babies." Tina smiled. "And while you're here, the doctors would like you to stay in bed as much as possible." She glanced at him. "Dad, you can come along. For security reasons, you'll have a matching armband."

His heart gave a funny little flip when she called him dad, assuming of course that he was the baby's father. He didn't correct her since he cared about the baby as much as he would if he were the biological father. He smiled and gently squeezed Ava's hand. "That would be great, thanks."

When Tina left, Ava whispered, "What about Zulu? Are you going to find another motel room for the night?"

"Maybe." He hesitated, then said, "I'll need to take her out soon, but that can wait until you're settled in the room."

"But what about later?"

He didn't want to lie, but he didn't want to worry Ava either. "Once darkness falls, I'm going to scope out the Death Rays' warehouse."

"By yourself?" Her blue eyes widened in alarm.

"Yes, but I need you to trust me, Ava. My SEAL training has prepared me for this. I really need to see if Callie is there."

She swallowed hard, then nodded. "Okay, but please be safe."

"Always." He didn't want to minimize the danger, yet he trusted in God's plan for him as well as his skill and training.

By the time they were settled in her hospital room, his stomach rumbled with hunger. He left just long enough to take Zulu outside, then returned to the second-floor hospital room.

"I'm getting hungry," Ava confessed.

He rang for the nurse. When she came in, he asked, "Is Ava on a special diet? We'd like to grab something for dinner."

"No special diet," the nurse, Carmen, assured her. She eyed Zulu warily, as did most of the hospital staff. Thankfully, no one put up a fuss. "But you may want to go easy on the salt. You can order a tray to be brought to your room."

"What if we wanted to grab a bite in the cafeteria?" Nico asked. "Is that okay?"

"Sure. I'll get a wheelchair," Carmen said.

"Wheelchair." Ava grimaced. "Ugh."

"No complaints." He took the wheelchair from Carmen. Zulu sniffed the seat area, as if suspicious of the device. "Thanks. I can handle it from here."

He helped Ava get into the chair, then wheeled her down to the cafeteria. It wasn't large, but they were able to get a variety of meals. Ava chose a chef's salad, while he grabbed a cheeseburger. Zulu curled up beneath the table at their feet.

He took both of her hands in his and bowed his head. "Dear Lord, we thank You for this meal and for keeping Ava and her baby safe in Your care. Please continue to protect them both. Amen."

"Amen," Ava murmured. Maybe it was his imagination, but she seemed reluctant to release his hands. "Thank you, Nico. That was heartfelt."

"You're welcome." He didn't need her gratitude, but he was pleased she'd participated in the prayer. "God is always there for you, Ava. All you have to do is believe."

"I know." She surprised him by smiling and nodding. "I've started praying again."

"I'm glad to hear that." When they were finished eating, he wheeled Ava back to her room. After helping her to bed, he stepped back. "I should go. Zulu needs to go out, and I have work to do."

"Will you call me?" She reached for the phone at the side of the bed. "Take this number and give me yours."

He dutifully wrote his cell number on a paper towel, then programmed her hospital number into his phone. "I'll call you, but I'll also have my phone on silent. Especially once I'm close to the warehouse. Don't call me unless it's an emergency, okay?"

"I won't." She kept the paper towel under her phone. "I feel better just having a way to contact you."

"Good." He made a mental note to buy another disposable phone for her. "Your only job is to rest and relax, understand?"

"Yes." She grimaced and gestured at the TV. "I'll find something to watch, although I haven't had a television in a long time, so I have no clue what's available anymore."

It made his heart ache to know how she'd lived these past eight months. He leaned down to press a kiss to her forehead, but she lifted her head up so their mouths met. For a moment, their lips clung, then he found himself kissing her the way he'd always wanted.

And she didn't push him away.

He reluctantly broke off their kiss, fighting to control his breathing. He'd imagined kissing Ava, but not like this, when she was in the hospital and he was headed out to find her kidnapped friend. "I'll see you soon."

"Be safe, Nico," she said as he stepped back from the bed. "Zulu too."

"We will." He gave her a nod, then turned and quickly left with Zulu at his side. It was harder than he'd anticipated to walk away. Granted, he knew she was safer here in the hospital than anywhere else.

It still wasn't easy to switch gears. To focus his mind on the mission before him.

Nico's first stop was to pick up a high-powered camera, a disposable phone for Ava, grease paint to use on his face and hands, and a pack of zip ties.

He'd debated leaving Zulu with Ava but figured that would send the hospital staff off the deep end. Keeping her in the SUV with the windows open partway would have to be good enough for the time being. He wasn't planning to leave her until the sun was down, and by then, the temperature inside the vehicle shouldn't get too high.

And he'd go back and check on her as often as he could. Hopefully, he could get into position, take the photos he needed, then get out of there within a reasonable amount of time. A plan that would depend on his getting a glimpse of Callie.

He hated the idea of bringing the entire team in to infiltrate the motorcycle gang's warehouse if Callie wasn't being held here. That sort of mission was high risk, considering these guys were armed and dangerous. No reason to put his happily married teammates in harm's way if he couldn't verify there was a hostage to rescue.

After spending what was left of the lingering daylight with Zulu outside, he tucked her into the back of the SUV and drove around to find a new parking spot. He didn't want to use the previous location. Besides, he needed to get closer.

Earlier that day, he'd noticed a dilapidated and seemingly abandoned building not far from the warehouse that would suit his needs. He took a moment to check the place out using his binoculars, searching specifically for cameras. From there, he couldn't see any, but he'd check again when he was closer.

He drove past the warehouse, then turned to park alongside the building. He chose the side of the structure that was farthest away from the Death Rays' warehouse. Using his binoculars, he scoured the place for cameras but didn't find any. Then he slid out of the car to make sure the building was empty.

The only things living inside were vermin and bugs. He wasn't fond of either, but he easily ignored them. Looking up, he noticed several holes in the roof that made him think the place would collapse in a brisk wind.

Or go up like a match if there was even a hint of a spark.

Satisfied this location would work as a staging spot, he patiently slid back into the SUV and waited until quarter to midnight to make his move. He would normally wait until the middle of the night, but he couldn't ignore the need to get back to Ava as soon as possible. Looping the camera strap around his neck, he smeared the face paint on, then eased out of the SUV.

Game time.

Armed with both his Sig Sauer and MK 3 knife, he made his way past the dilapidated building to the next one. A quick glance around proved there were cameras on the outside of that building.

He slowly made his way closer, knowing many cameras were motion activated. During his time with the SEAL teams, they'd learned how to trick the cameras by moving with excruciating stealth. It took a lot of time and patience, but as the minutes ticked by without hearing any type of alarm being raised, he felt certain his plan had worked.

There was only one window on this side of the structure. He continued inching his way toward it, keeping in the shadows. There was no light shining from within, either because it was blacked out or because the place was empty.

With extreme caution, he looked through the window. It wasn't blacked out by paint or boards, but the interior was empty. It looked to be a storage facility, based on the numerous boxes and crates.

He would have loved to know what was being stored inside, but his priority was to find Callie, so he moved on.

As he rounded the rear of the building, he could hear

voices coming from the next warehouse. According to Ava, that was the main one Simon used as a headquarters.

Earlier he'd noticed at least forty motorcycles parked out front, but now he could see four big bikes sitting outside the back doorway. Maybe belonging to Simon and a few of his trusted thugs. He waited for several minutes to see if anyone would come searching for him, but the area was quiet.

Good. He hoped and prayed it would stay that way.

There were a few more windows in this warehouse, so he continued moving slowly toward the closest one. The voices from inside the warehouse grew louder, and he realized the window was open.

Interesting development. He pressed himself against the side of the building and strained to listen. A few guys were discussing their plans for the next day, which included making a big delivery. When he didn't hear anything about Ava or Callie, he moved on to the next window.

After a solid hour of moving stealthily from one location to the next, he feared he'd never find Callie. He hated to admit the possibility that Callie was already dead.

Determined not to leave without knowing the truth, he inched his way to the other side of the building. It wasn't easy to move slowly past the motorcycles parked out back, but he managed to make it without tripping the cameras.

The first window looked to be a bedroom. His pulse kicked up as he wondered if all the bedrooms were on this side of the warehouse. He crept toward the next window and peeked inside.

A woman was curled up on the bed, short, dark hair falling over her pale face. Her eyes were closed, her cheek badly bruised. His gaze traveled down to note one ankle was bound to the bed frame.

Callie.

He took a moment to consider his options. Getting her out of the room wouldn't be easy, there was only one of him and countless Death Rays members. He hated to leave her there, but he knew it was best. He slowly brought up the camera and took several pictures. He planned to use this to elicit support from Bryce.

Nico had what he'd come for, but he still needed to make his way back to the SUV where Zulu was waiting patiently for his return. He took a moment to remove the memory card from the camera, in case he needed to ditch it, then retraced his steps.

It was far more difficult now to move slowly. He forced himself to count off in his mind with each step he made. As he came to the corner of the building where he'd have to get past the four motorcycles, he heard two voices.

"How are we going to use her as bait when we can't get through to Ava?" one guy asked. "We need a new plan, Simon."

The glow of a cigarette burned in the darkness. "I have my sources. I know where she is. I'll have her back here very soon to accept the punishment she deserves."

Every muscle in Nico's body tensed. Was Simon bluffing? Or did he really know where Ava was? Even if Simon somehow knew Ava was in the hospital, it was unlikely he could get to her, considering the security on the OB ward. Yet Nico's training had taught him nothing was impossible.

Nico silently slipped the memory card back into the camera, raised it, and took several photos of the two men. They wouldn't be great without a flash, but hopefully better than nothing. When that was finished, he once again shoved the memory card deep into his pocket for safekeeping.

He wanted nothing more than to get out of there, but he

didn't dare move from this location with Simon and his buddy standing outside the back door to the building and motion cameras all around him.

His only option was to wait them out, hoping and praying Ava was safe inside the hospital.

---

THE HOURS HAD PASSED SLOWLY. Ava decided she didn't much care for most of what was on the television, obviously she hadn't missed anything in the time she'd been gone. She'd slept on and off for several hours, getting more rest than she'd ever had in the past six months.

And while she was thrilled her blood pressure was now normal, she didn't like being in the hospital. The bed wasn't comfortable, and despite her room being at the end of a hallway, she could still hear babies crying on occasion. A preview, she knew, of what she'd face in approximately two months.

Or less.

The walls of the room felt as if they were closing in on her. The room was small, and when she'd tried the window, it wouldn't open. She occasionally experienced bouts of claustrophobia since the night Simon had tried to strangle her.

It seemed this was one of those times.

The fact that she hadn't heard anything from Nico bothered her. Yet she also didn't dare call him for fear of putting him in danger. Feeling helpless, she prayed for his safety and that he'd find Callie alive and unharmed.

At one in the morning, she abruptly woke up, her heart thudding against her ribs. Had she heard something? It wasn't a crying baby, but maybe a noise?

Had Nico returned? Possibly. Now that she was awake, she needed to use the bathroom. When she finished, she straightened her white nightgown—the nursing staff had mentioned that she could wear whatever was most comfortable—plopped into the wheelchair, and scooted toward the door.

Peering out, she could see the dimly lit hallway was empty. The lights were able to be dimmed in deference to the hour. The nursing staff needed to be able to see after all. She'd noticed they'd used a small light near the door when coming in to check on her rather than the bright fluorescent bulbs overhead.

No sign of Nico or Zulu. She tried to squelch a flash of disappointment.

Now that she was up, she knew going back to sleep would be useless. She wheeled herself out into the hall, heading up to the nurse's station.

There wasn't anyone sitting behind the desk, the staff must all be busy in various patient rooms. Obviously, women in labor came in at all hours of the day and night.

Jayne kicked and rolled in her belly, making her smile. She didn't like being confined to the wheelchair but made the best of it as she turned to head back down to her room.

Then she paused, realizing she was hungry again. There had been vending machines in the cafeteria, hadn't there? She wheeled back to her room and rummaged in her backpack for cash. She didn't keep it in her purse and was glad to note she had about a week's worth of pay in there. Not a fortune by any means but a little over four hundred dollars.

Still, she hesitated to use even a fraction of that simply to get something to eat. This was the only money she'd have from now until the baby was born. Nico hadn't let her pay for anything so far, but did she really want to live off his generosity indefinitely?

Nope.

She thought about the money she'd drained from her savings account after escaping from Simon. She still had some money squirreled away, but she had been determined to keep it for a true emergency.

Being hungry in the middle of the night wasn't an emergency.

Fine. She wouldn't get something to eat. But maybe she'd head down there anyway for something to do. A change of scenery would be welcome.

Ava wheeled herself out of the room, and this time, a woman was sitting behind the desk. "I'd like to head down to the cafeteria," she said.

"Okay, that's fine." Without hesitation, the nurse pushed the button to let her out the main door. Ava had been impressed with how the unit was locked to protect the babies from being abducted.

The door opened, and she wheeled herself down the hall to the elevator. The cafeteria was on the first floor, so it only took a few minutes for the elevator to get to the main level.

As she exited the elevator, she could see an older man dressed in a security guard uniform sitting behind the front desk. He looked up when she rolled past, giving her a nod in acknowledgment. She smiled and continued toward the cafeteria.

The vending machines were on the opposite side of the room from where the regular meals were served. The main service area was closed now, cordoned off with a wire gate.

Surprisingly, the room was vacant. Apparently, the staff

didn't congregate down there during their shifts. Or maybe they took their breaks earlier or later.

With a shrug, she decided to check out the vending machines. She wheeled her way over and perused the offerings.

Honestly, the main features didn't look very appetizing. She wrinkled her nose, thinking it was best to avoid eating something that was high in salt or that might make her feel sick.

Humiliating enough to have thrown up in front of Nico.

The vending machine farther down offered a variety of snacks. The chocolate looked good, but it was an indulgence she didn't need.

Funny how being on the run for your life and hiding from sight could bring things into perspective. She winced at how she'd thought her life as a dental hygienist was boring and mundane.

She'd gladly take boring and mundane over the way she'd spent the past seven months. Constantly looking over her shoulder and on the move. Looking for new jobs with those who didn't ask too many questions and paid in cash.

She smoothed a hand over her belly, wanting more for her child. Which was part of the reason she'd hoped to head to Mexico once the baby was born.

Having been diagnosed with a mild form of preeclampsia only made that plan more complicated. If her baby was born early, she'd need to stay in the US for additional medical care.

Medical care despite having no insurance. She winced and began to wheel her chair backward out of the vending area. This wasn't the time to worry about that. Maybe she'd be able to carry her baby to term.

And he or she wouldn't need any medical care.

She drew in a deep breath and let it out slowly. *No stress, remember?* She could almost hear Nico telling her that God would protect her and the baby.

She felt someone come up behind her. Assuming it was the security guard from the front desk, she said, "Oh, let me get out of your way."

But when she tried to move the chair back, she couldn't move. Twisting in her seat wasn't easy, but she tried to glance over her shoulder to see who was back there.

Her chest tightened as she saw a tall man wearing motorcycle gear, including a leather vest. No, it couldn't be. This had to be a coincidence.

"Found you," he said.

She opened her mouth to scream, then felt something hard poke against the back of the chair. She froze, her heart pounding so hard she could imagine her blood pressure soaring sky high.

"Scream and I'll shoot. At this range, I can't miss. You and your brat will die."

Ava fought to remain calm. "What do you want?"

"It's not what I want." The biker dude bent down, forcing her to turn away from his rancid cigarette breath. "It's what Simon wants. And that's you."

How was it possible that Simon's thugs had found her there? Had they known she was in the hospital? Had they been keeping an eye out for her to leave the locked obstetrics unit? Another foolish decision had backfired in the worst way.

The biker pulled her wheelchair back and turned her so that she was facing the doorway. She didn't feel the gun poking her in the back as he used both hands to steer the wheelchair.

He pushed her out of the cafeteria and toward the front

door. She stared at the security guard, trying to catch his gaze, but he didn't seem to notice the angst on her face as she was casually rolled away.

For a moment, she considered screaming. Would this biker dude really shoot her here in front of the security guard?

Maybe, after all, he'd have plenty of time to shoot her, and the guard, then escape since the area was otherwise deserted.

She continued staring toward the security guard, begging him to notice her.

But then she was outside in the cool night air, being steered toward a car that was waiting near the curb.

She closed her eyes in despair, realizing she would be taken straight to Simon.

And this time, Simon would make sure she never escaped again.

# CHAPTER EIGHT

Nico frowned as he approached the hospital. Was that Ava being pushed in a wheelchair toward a waiting car? He instinctively reached for his weapon, then stopped. Ava wouldn't go with a biker without a reason.

He felt certain this guy had taken her out at gunpoint, the same way Callie had been taken a little over twenty-four hours ago. If that was the case, Nico didn't dare startle the guy into shooting.

Instead, he slowly drove past, his gut clenching as he noticed Ava being placed in the back seat, wearing what appeared to be her white nightgown. He swallowed hard and quickly memorized the license plate of the vehicle. When he was out of view, he quickly turned the SUV to follow. The car had already pulled away from the curb. He needed to stay back far enough, which wasn't too difficult because he knew where they were going.

Simon's warehouse.

He used the hands-free function to call Bryce. The phone rang several times before he heard a sleepy, "This better be good, Nico."

"Ava has been kidnapped by the Death Rays, and they also have a woman named Callie they're holding hostage. I have a van plate number, I need you to run it for me."

"You're serious? Hang on." Bryce didn't sound sleepy anymore. "Give me the number, I'll get a BOLO out for it."

Nico sensed it would be too late, that the driver of the car would get to the warehouse before any cop could spot and stop him. But he recited the plate number anyway.

"I'm following them," he told Bryce. "I was able to confirm Callie is being held at the warehouse too; her ankle is cuffed to a bed."

"Not good," Bryce said. He'd put the call on speaker, and Nico could hear clothes rustling as Bryce got dressed. "Kirby and I will meet you there."

"Hold on, Ava's pregnant, we're not going in guns blazing."

"Pregnant?" He heard Bryce groan. "That does complicate things."

"You have no idea. They kidnapped Ava from the hospital." A locked ward, which gave him pause. "She's supposed to be on bed rest. If her blood pressure gets too high, she could have seizures and lose the baby." He desperately wished he'd have asked Mason and the others to come earlier. "Meet me at the Gas N Go station on Curtis Street. We need a plan to get both Ava and Callie out of there safely."

"Got it." Bryce disconnected from the call.

Despite the early hour, Nico didn't hesitate to call Mason. "What's wrong?" his senior chief asked.

"I need you and the other guys to get to LA as soon as possible." Nico strove to sound calm, but inside he was anything but. Ava's life and that of her unborn child were in jeopardy, and he'd never been so afraid in his entire life.

Except maybe that last op where he and the others had performed CPR on Jaydon. The same feeling of helplessness had hit him hard then too. "Simon is part of the Desert Death Rays motorcycle gang, and he just kidnapped Ava from the hospital."

"We can be there soon," Mason promised.

It may not be soon enough, but Nico had only himself to blame. He thought about the three guys who'd approached them yesterday. They must have been paid by Simon to report anything suspicious.

"Ava's pregnant and could lose the baby," he said in a rush. "She's not supposed to be stressed and has been kidnapped at gunpoint. I know you're four hours away, and the other guys are even farther, except for Kaleb, but I need you, Senior Chief. It's bad." His voice hitched. "Really bad."

"Dallas, Hudd, and Dawson are actually here in town," Mason said, his voice calm.

"They are?" He was flabbergasted. "How?"

"I called them yesterday, and they decided not to wait. We knew this day would come, and we're ready to get Ava back. I'll have Kaleb meet you immediately. The rest of us be coming in via chopper, so we can get there faster."

"Thank you. Tell Kaleb to meet me at the Gas N Go on Curtis Street. I have another cop friend meeting me there too. We'll begin a plan of attack."

"Good, we'll bring extra gear, including vests. The chopper I've lined up is former military, he won't give us any trouble."

"You've thought of everything, haven't you?" Nico managed a grim smile as he drove, keeping an eye on the car carrying Ava roughly five car lengths ahead of him. This was God's plan. The Lord had sent his friends when he needed them the most. The vehicle ahead of him abruptly turned. He straightened in his seat, his heart pounding. "Mason, I gotta go."

Nico gripped the steering wheel tightly, trying to understand where the car was headed. He made the same turn, then realized this was a shortcut to reach the back of Simon's warehouse. He quickly stopped the car and shifted into reverse. He didn't need to follow them the rest of the way.

Nico knew the back of the warehouse very well. That was where he'd patiently waited for Simon and his buddy to finish smoking so that he could get out of there. Even then, it had taken him a painstakingly long time to move along the building to avoid tripping the cameras and getting caught.

He'd made it back to the SUV where Zulu waited in the back. He'd hurried toward the hospital, only to discover he'd been ten minutes too late.

Ten minutes!

There wasn't anything he could do to change the current situation, so he ruthlessly shoved the guilt aside. It had been reasonable to expect Ava to be safe in the hospital. Yet he hadn't anticipated the Hispanic guys being a part of Simon's lookout program either.

His fault for underestimating Simon's power and wide reach. But again, rehashing his mistakes wouldn't help Ava now. He needed to stay calm and think. He wasn't alone in this situation. Bryce would meet him, as would Kaleb and the others.

They'd create a plan to rescue Ava, getting her back safely without any harm to her baby. Callie too.

Failure was not an option. Again, those moments he and

the others had performed CPR on Jaydon while in the water, swimming to their pickup point, flashed in his mind.

He'd prayed then, too, but Jaydon hadn't made it.

He desperately needed to believe God would spare Ava and her baby. *Please, Lord, please keep Ava, her baby, and Callie safe in Your care!*

After backing up, he turned and drove straight to the gas station. Thankfully, Bryce was already there waiting, his K9, Kirby, sitting tall beside him. His buddy was dressed in black jeans and a black shirt, and he wore a black bandanna over his light blond hair.

"Nico," Bryce said by way of greeting. "What's the plan?"

Nico jumped out of the SUV, then let Zulu out too. He felt guilty for keeping the dog cooped up inside for so long, but now he led her over to a grassy area to do her business. When she finished, he returned to where Bryce waited. The dogs sniffed each other with interest, then Nico commanded Zulu to stay. "My entire SEAL team will be joining us as soon as possible. In the meantime, we need to come up with a plan."

Bryce frowned. "This should be a SWAT team police op."

Nico knew his buddy was right. Technically, he and his SEAL teammates didn't have any jurisdiction here. But he knew how the SWAT team would handle this. They'd surround the warehouse and set up a hostage negotiator. They'd have sharpshooters stationed on the roof looking for a clear shot to kill Simon and whoever else was holding the women.

The problem was there were too many bikers, and they were all armed. In his humble opinion, the likelihood of getting Ava and Callie out alive with a SWAT team response were slim to none.

Emphasis on none.

Simon would kill them. Or one of his trigger-happy, possibly drugged-up biker buddies would. After all, this was about revenge. To punish Ava for killing Banjo. There would be no reason for Simon to keep her or Callie alive for much longer.

And that was a risk he was unwilling to take.

"Bryce, you were a Navy SEAL too. You know that a team of former SEALs can infiltrate the warehouse to rescue the hostages better than a SWAT team can. We'll use stealth and military tactics rather than following police procedure, with hostage negotiators and sharpshooters. They may even try to get the Feds involved, but that will take time that we can't spare."

Bryce held his gaze for a long moment, then sighed. "Yeah, I know. But if my boss finds out I was a part of this, I'll lose my job."

"You don't have to be a part of it," Nico assured him. "In fact, I'd rather have you out here to be a liaison with the local police. The moment someone starts shooting, it won't take long for cops to swarm the place."

"No way. I'm not sitting out there while you guys do the dirty work." Bryce narrowed his green eyes stubbornly. "Not happening. I'm going in with you and the others."

Nico hesitated. It wasn't that he didn't want Bryce's help, at this point he'd take anything he could get. Yet they weren't the SEALs they were before. "There's something you should know. We're not all functioning at a hundred percent. We were injured on our last op, some worse than others. Mason is deaf in one ear and partially deaf in another, although he recently underwent a cochlear implant surgery, which has helped immensely. Hudd is blind in one eye and gets debilitating headaches. Dawson took a gut load of shrapnel, although he's doing much better now. Dallas had shoulder reconstruction surgery, Kaleb has a new knee, and I tore my Achilles tendon. We're determined not to let any of these injuries hold us back, but you need to understand we're not a fully functional team. At least, not the way we were in our prime."

"I hear you, but I'd rather stay with you, injured or not. I trust our training over that of the local police any day of the week." There was no hesitation in Bryce's voice. Then he added, "I didn't escape unscathed either."

"None of us did," Nico softly agreed. "I still think you're better suited to stay out here as our liaison."

An SUV pulled up beside Nico's vehicle. When he saw Kaleb's face and the black lab in the back crate, he couldn't help but smile. Having his teammate there already helped him feel better about the monumental task before them.

"Kaleb, this is LAPD Officer Bryce Flynn and his K9, Kirby. Bryce, Kaleb Tyson and his black lab, Sierra."

Zulu and Sierra sniffed at each other curiously, no doubt remembering when they'd all been together to pick up the puppies at Lillian's rescue. The three men had to work to keep the three dogs in line. They were well trained, but they were still dogs.

"You're former Navy too, aren't you?" Kaleb asked as the two men shook hands.

"Yes, but I got out sooner than you guys," Bryce said.

Kaleb nodded, and they would have likely talked more, if time wasn't of the essence. "Nico, bring me up to speed."

"I'm sure Mason told you most of it," Nico said. He gave an abbreviated version, then said, "There is another warehouse next to the main one, which is where I saw Callie chained to her bed. I believe Simon's intent was to use Callie to draw Ava out, but she left her phone behind, so that never happened."

"Jerk," Kaleb said. "How many bikers total?"

"At least forty, likely more." Nico refused to let the number of hostiles mess with his head. They'd been in worse situations, and despite the fact that they were on US soil rather than the mountains of Afghanistan, this wouldn't be any different.

Nico led the way to a dusty section of the concrete and crouched to draw a rough map of the warehouse as he'd seen it earlier. Zulu stretched out on the ground beside him. "There are a couple of bedrooms in the main warehouse along the farthest wall." Nico gestured to the area. "But there may be other bedrooms on the other side, I didn't get a chance to check every window. Oh, and there are motion cameras all over the place."

"Great," Bryce muttered.

"We can circumvent them," Kaleb said.

"I already have, that's how I verified Callie was being held here," Nico agreed. "It's time-consuming, but that's nothing new."

"How do you want us to approach?" Bryce asked.

Nico glanced at his watch. The hour was five past two in the morning. He didn't want to wait too much longer before going in. They needed to move soon, to use the darkness to their advantage.

Besides, most of the Desert Death Rays had to sleep sometime. They'd keep a few guys up on watch, but he knew the SEAL team could handle them.

"I'm not sure when Mason, Hudd, Dawson, and Dallas will get here," Nico said. "I'd feel better if we had the entire team available. We'll need three guys minimum to go in to get Ava and Callie. One man for each woman and a guy for cover. The others will need to eliminate the night guards and to provide backup as needed."

Kaleb looked at his watch. "Mason and the gang should be here soon."

Nico lifted a brow. "Even using a chopper means it will take them a while to get here."

"Roughly an hour, but they were ready to go when you called." A ghost of a smile creased Kaleb's features. "They were planning to come today regardless. You just moved the timeline up a bit. Mason said it would take about an hour to get to LA, and thankfully, there's not much traffic at this hour of the morning."

"They had the chopper set up ahead of time?" Nico was humbled by the news. "I had no idea."

"Yeah, well, we knew that when you found Ava, we may need to move. And if she wasn't in danger, then we all wanted to meet her." Kaleb's grin faded. "I pray we get that chance."

"We will." Nico infused confidence in his voice. "We have to."

He hadn't gone into detail about Ava's preeclampsia. There was no point in harping on it. Getting her safely away from Simon was their core mission. From there, they could take her right back to the hospital to make sure the baby was okay.

But that didn't stop him from praying.

Kaleb's phone rang. "Chief, what's your ETA? Forty-five minutes? Got it." His buddy disconnected from the call. "They'll be here shortly before three o'clock."

That was better than he'd hoped. He pointed to the warehouse he'd drawn in the dust. "We'll have seven guys, total. I plan to be one of the three that goes in to get Ava. I'll need a guy on each of the four sides of the building." He marked the locations. "The goal will be to take out any and all guards."

"I'll go with you," Bryce offered.

"Me too," Kaleb said.

He was honored to have such good friends. Guys who would walk into danger beside you to rescue someone they barely knew.

"Thank you." He cleared his throat. "Mason and the rest of the team are bringing vests and additional weapons. But they won't have their dogs. We probably can't take ours either. Not even Kirby, who is technically the only fully trained police K9," he added wryly.

"From what I can see, your dogs are trained well enough," Bryce said. "But the dogs might cause a problem with the motion sensor cameras."

"Exactly my fear. We'll plan to make our move as soon as we're geared up and ready to roll."

"Sounds good," Bryce agreed.

Kaleb nodded.

Nico stared down at the map, visualizing the sections of the warehouse he'd been able to glimpse through the window.

If all went as planned, they'd infiltrate the warehouse at roughly three fifteen or three thirty in the morning. His goal was to get Callie and Ava out of there before the rest of the Desert Death Rays knew they were gone.

God willing, this would all be over very soon with no casualties for his team. Or for the hostages.

He didn't relish killing anyone, but he wasn't going to lose any sleep over losing a few of the bikers.

Nico would do whatever was necessary to get Ava and Callie out of there, knowing God would forgive him.

---

AVA HAD BEEN FORCED to confront Simon by the man who'd abducted her from the hospital. She had felt the gun in her back as he forced her to walk from the car to the warehouse.

It took every ounce of willpower to remain calm, praying her blood pressure wouldn't go sky high again and risk harming her baby.

"Why didn't you tell me I was going to be a father?" Simon had asked, a creepy grin spreading over his features.

"I didn't think you'd care." She'd kept her tone even, knowing Simon didn't like it when she became angry or emotional. He'd wanted a robot woman, one who would take his abuse without protest. Someone who would cower and cave to every one of his demands.

"Oh, I care, Ava. Or should I call you Renee?" He tsked. "It's so hard to keep all your various aliases straight."

A cold chill rippled over her. Simon had been closer than she'd realized if he'd known of her different aliases. In that moment, she knew God had brought Nico to protect her in the nick of time. "What do you want, Simon?"

"You killed Banjo." All hint of humor vanished, and his icy gaze raked over her. "And for that you must pay."

"I didn't mean to kill him," she said, trying not to show how scared she was. Simon had always been unpredictable. His moods would swing from one end of the spectrum to the next without warning.

"The camera doesn't lie," he shot back.

"I knew you were the one who sent me those pictures."

She kept her voice level rather than accusatory. "But you must know they don't tell the whole story."

"I'll make sure there are plenty of witnesses to testify against you." He waved a hand. "And I have those pictures along with a real-time video of the entire murder in a place you'll never find them. Oh, and just so you're aware, I've added more cameras in the months you've been gone." He grinned again. "No one will get close without me seeing them."

She'd assumed as much and knew Nico had been prepared for the cameras too. "Speaking of cameras, the hospital is going to know something terrible happened to me. They have security cameras too, or didn't your stupid biker thug mention that?" The moment the taunt left her mouth she wished she hadn't said it.

Simon slapped her with enough force to send her flying sideways onto the bed. Pain shot through her face, leaving her breathless. She instinctively curled into a ball, desperate to protect her baby.

"That biker thug is Abe. He's Banjo's brother," Simon hissed. "You better have some respect, he hates you more than I do." Simon poked at her with the tip of his gun. "And I bet he'd love to hurt you and that brat the exact same way you killed Banjo."

The image of Abe stabbing her stomach made her want to scream. Somehow, she managed to hold it back, but she mentally braced for another blow, certain that if Simon continued to beat her, she'd lose the baby.

*Please, Lord. Please keep my baby safe in Your care!*

Tears welled in her eyes as she tried to anticipate where Simon would strike next. Only he didn't.

"Simon? There's a problem with the incoming shipment," someone said. "You need to get down there right away."

"I'll be back," Simon had threatened before leaving her alone in the room.

Swallowing hard, she gingerly sat up, pushing her hair from her face. Her cheek throbbed with pain, and she tasted the metallic blood from where her lip had been split, but she ignored both injuries, taking a moment to smooth her hands over her belly to soothe the baby.

"Low blood pressure," she whispered. "Stay calm, there's nothing to be afraid of. Nico will find us."

It took several minutes for her to get her emotions under control. Praying helped keep her grounded. She stood and walked to the door, unsurprised to find it was locked. She turned and made her way back to the cot.

When she'd been thrust into the car by Abe, she'd thought she'd seen Nico's SUV, but she made a point not to look at it too long so Abe wouldn't get suspicious. Even if the SUV wasn't Nico's, he'd probably know she was gone from the hospital by now. The nursing staff had taken his phone number as her point of contact since she didn't have a phone.

Nico would find her, but where was Callie? She wondered if Nico had found Callie while he'd been checking the warehouse.

Glancing around the small, spartan bedroom, she imagined Callie might be nearby in a similar space. Simon hadn't bothered to tie her up, likely assuming she wouldn't be able to escape so easily this time, being eight months pregnant.

And he'd be right. A wave of despair washed over her. She didn't even have her knife, it was still in her backpack. She'd grown lax being with Nico. Normally, she would have taken it everywhere.

She stood and began searching beneath the bed, hoping to find something she could use as a weapon. But the room was completely empty except for the bare mattress on the cot. There wasn't a pillow or any sheets either. Nothing that she could use against Simon or one of his biker thugs.

Okay, then. She'd have to wait for Nico to come. And she knew in her heart he would. She wished she'd allowed him to call in his SEAL friends and his cop buddy sooner. And for a moment, she remembered their kiss. The one she'd initiated.

Looking around her prison room now, she couldn't regret having kissed Nico. He was here out of duty, but she'd come to care about him.

Maybe even falling in love with him.

It was probably just the danger surrounding them, but she didn't think so. After the time she'd spent with Simon, especially the way he'd just treated her, she understood just how different Nico was.

A man who was strong but also a gentleman. A man of honor, of bravery. He was the kind of man any woman would be lucky to have.

Too bad she didn't deserve his love. Nico was a man of God, he'd already forgiven her foolish decisions, the sins she'd committed. He'd come for her because she was Jaydon's little sister.

But that didn't mean he loved her. Not in the way that truly mattered.

Her stomach churned with nausea, and she became aware of a nagging headache, a different pain from the throbbing in her cheek.

A wave of fear washed over her. This was exactly how she'd felt when she was in the car with Nico, shortly before she'd thrown up.

No, please. Not now. She couldn't have another episode now.

She curled up along the side of the bare mattress and began to take long, deep breaths to bring her blood pressure down. Slow and easy. It had worked once in the hospital, so it had to work again. She could do this.

She had no choice but to do this.

# CHAPTER NINE

Nico looked at the concerned faces of his teammates. He'd seen them frequently over the months after they'd all been given an honorable medical discharge from the Navy, but this was the first time they'd work together since their last op. The one that had gone seriously sideways, killing Jaydon and wounding all of them.

Now they were just as determined to rescue Jaydon's sister, Ava. And the young woman Callie Burgess. Every one of them would put their own life on the line to protect the innocent.

And that included K9 Officer Bryce Flynn.

"Any last questions?" Nico asked as he tightened the strap of his bullet-resistant vest.

"We're good," Mason answered for all of them.

The goal was for them to get in and out with the women without any of the Desert Death Rays realizing what had happened.

A task easier said than done, but nothing they hadn't faced before.

"Chief, you, Hudd, Dawson, and Dallas take each of

the four sides of the building," Nico repeated. Mason was their senior chief, but he was the one in charge of this op. It seemed strange, but he was the one who knew the layout and what to expect going in. Thankfully, they were geared up, Mason had even brought earpiece radios for them to use. "When you've cleared those areas, Bryce, Kaleb, and I will go in to find the women."

"Roger that," Dallas drawled. "Let's do this."

Nico nodded, then added, "Thank you. For coming to help."

"No need, this is what we're trained for." Mason gestured toward the warehouse. "Let's move."

It bothered Nico that these men putting themselves in danger had wives and in some cases children waiting for them back home. If anything happened to them, he'd be the one responsible for the loss.

Nico quickly thrust those thoughts aside. His team was here voluntarily, and they were experts at infiltrating the enemy. He trusted in God and in their individual training. Better to stay focused on the mission.

The SEAL mantra—the only easy day was yesterday—was appropriate here.

He crouched near the warehouse that appeared to be used by the Death Rays for storage of who knew what with Bryce and Kaleb. Together as a team, they'd decided against using their respective K9s. In their SEAL ops, they'd sometimes used one dog to track the scent of a tango, but tonight, it wasn't reasonable to go into hostile territory with three dogs. Especially not with motion cameras everywhere.

Mason, Hudd, Dallas, and Dawson hadn't brought their K9s because the chopper wasn't large enough to accommodate that many people and their dogs. Nico had put Zulu in the back of the SUV. Kaleb and Bryce had done the same.

Nico couldn't deny feeling a bit lost without Zulu at his side, but he knew it was for the best. Stealth was key. They couldn't be hampered by dogs on leashes, and leaving them off leash would only put them in harm's way.

Even if the cameras weren't a concern, too many unknown variables awaited them inside the warehouse.

The radio in Nico's ear remained silent as the four men slowly crept into position. Patience was a virtue, but knowing Ava and her unborn child were in danger, not just from Simon and his men but from the possibility of going into full-blown eclampsia, was impossible to ignore.

Straining to listen, he was reassured when there was nothing but silence from the main warehouse. He knew the guys would take out their guards without making a sound.

Finally, he heard a low voice in his ear; it was Mason. "South side secure, one tango down."

"West side secure, two tangos down," Dawson said.

"North side secure, one tango down," Dallas echoed.

"East side secure, one tango down," Hudd said. "The first room is empty, the second and third are occupied by women. Fourth room has a man sleeping inside."

"We're going in," Nico murmured, then gave the go signal to Kaleb and Bryce. The first phase of the mission was a success.

Time to implement the second phase, with a similar result.

Nico led the way, with Bryce behind him and Kaleb covering their six. As earlier that night, he moved with excruciating slowness as to not set off the motion cameras. They passed Dallas and the single biker that was sitting slumped against the side of the building. Nico barely glanced at the fallen man, his attention riveted on getting inside the building.

There was no doubt in his mind that this was the most dangerous aspect of the plan. He carefully eased the door open just enough to see inside the warehouse, listening intently.

All was quiet.

He slipped through the doorway, taking a moment to pull down his night vision goggles. He was in what appeared to be a main gathering room, with tables and chairs. No sign of any men, sleeping or otherwise. He stepped farther into the room, not as worried about cameras now, using hand signals to let the other two men know it was safe to enter.

Then he pointed to the left, reminding Kaleb and Bryce that was where he'd seen Callie being held in one of the bedrooms. A fact recently verified by Hudd. Passing through the doorway, Nico found himself in a long, narrow hallway with several doors along the left side.

It was an odd setup, almost as if the bedrooms had been an afterthought. And maybe the additional rooms had been. Based on Hudd's intel, he tested the door to the second and third rooms.

They were both locked.

It was what they'd expected, but it would still take time to breach if they were to escape without being seen or heard. As tempting as it was to simply blast through each doorway, Nico took up a position near the third room, leaving the second room to Bryce. They needed to work silently so as not to raise the alarm of the man sleeping in the fourth room.

From when he'd seen Callie earlier, he'd known what sort of door locks to expect. Nothing super industrial, thankfully. These areas hadn't been originally set up to keep people inside against their will.

He and Bryce went to work using screwdrivers to remove the door handles. Kaleb took up a defensive position in front of the fourth door in case the sleeping man became a threat.

Nico silently removed the door handle and carefully pushed the door open. His heart lodged in his throat when he saw Ava curled up in a ball, her back to the door as if attempting to protect her baby.

He crept into the room, knowing this was the most dangerous part of the mission. If Ava screamed in fear, she'd wake the guy sleeping on the other side of the wall.

"Ava, it's Nico." He whispered the words as he slipped his hand around her head to cover her mouth.

She immediately stiffened and lashed out with her legs.

"Shh. It's Nico." He whispered the words into her ear. "You need to stay quiet."

The tension eased from her body. Her eyes were wide and bright with tears. She nodded, and he removed his hand, then helped her into a sitting position. She stood, then wrapped her arms around his waist, leaning against him.

"We need to move very slowly and stay in the shadows," he whispered. "Motion cameras outside, understand?"

"Yes," she whispered, still leaning against him.

He wasn't sure if she was just weak from her ordeal or if she was feeling sick to her stomach again. Either way, getting her out of here should help. He gave her a quick hug, then pushed her behind him as he headed to the door.

Ava curled her fingers into the waistband of his jeans as if needing to maintain contact between them. He didn't mind a bit. He led Ava through the doorway and saw that Kaleb was there, waiting. Glancing over, he was relieved to see Bryce had Callie too. He was sure Bryce had warned the dark-haired woman about the motion cameras as she stood still at his side.

They weren't out of danger yet. Not by a long shot.

Nico continued leading the way, retracing their path down the narrow hall to the main room, then turning to head outside. Just as Nico stepped over the threshold, he heard a low warning in his ear.

"Second tango on the west," Dawson whispered. "He's down, but there could be more."

Nico's pulse kicked up at the thought of running into more Death Rays, but he stayed focused on getting Ava and Callie out of there. He slowly inched forward, glancing over at Dallas. His teammate gave a barely perceptible nod, encouraging him to keep going. He did so, knowing Kaleb, Dallas, and the others would continue to secure the building until the women were safely out of the line of fire.

He continued creeping carefully along the side of the building, toward the storage warehouse, which coincidentally was located on the west side of the building. When they finally made it to the corner, he eased around to find Dawson pressed up against the wall near two prone bodies. Again, Dawson gave a slight nod, and he continued inching forward, with Bryce and Callie hopefully mirroring his movements behind him.

Every cell in his body wanted to run, to hurry, but he didn't dare risk setting off an alarm. Not when they were so close.

He could feel Ava's tension as she did her best to copy his movements. He wished he could reassure her, but his senses were tuned to his surroundings. Still, when the voice spoke in his ear, he nearly jumped.

"Second tango down on the north," Dallas whispered.

Where were these guys coming from? He wasn't sure,

but there was nothing he could do but keep moving forward.

One slow inch at a time.

After what seemed like eons, he and Ava reached the storage warehouse. He didn't stop to wait for Bryce and Callie, he had to trust in the guy's skill to get Callie out of there safely.

He continued moving cautiously along the rear side of the storage building. They'd made it to the far corner when he heard another voice in his ear.

"Two tangos talking in the south doorway," Mason whispered. "Cover is blown. They're looking for the hostages."

"Roger," Nico said. Stealth instantly took a back seat to speed. He turned, swept Ava into his arms, and ran toward the SUVs. Behind him, he could tell Bryce had done the same with Callie. To their credit, both women didn't make a sound, despite how fearful they must have been.

He yanked open the car door and set Ava down so she could get inside. He shut the door, then ran around to get into the driver's seat. The plan all along had been to bug out if their cover was blown.

Now he needed to pray that the rest of the guys all made it without becoming injured or worse.

"Stay down," he told Ava, starting the engine. They needed to be ready to roll as soon as every last man was accounted for. In the rearview, he could see Callie and Bryce in his K9 vehicle, but there was no sign yet of Kaleb.

He held his breath knowing Kaleb would have hung back to help the other guys get clear.

Then suddenly the guys burst around the corner, all five running fast. Nico sent up a brief prayer of thanks as the men instinctively headed toward various SUVs. His three teammates joined Kaleb in his SUV, leaving Hudd to get into his vehicle. Bryce and Callie were already inside his police SUV. The moment Hudd's backside hit the leather, Nico punched the accelerator, pulling out of the gas station parking lot and out onto the road.

In the rearview, he saw that the other two SUVs, Kaleb's and Bryce's, soon followed suit.

They split up heading off in different directions, fully expecting multiple biker guys to follow. Nico used his radio, glad they were still all wired for sound.

"I'm taking Ava to the closest hospital, rendezvous there when you're clear."

A chorus of "roger that" echoed in his ear. Hudd simply nodded from the back seat.

"The same hospital as before?" Ava asked, fear in her gaze. "That's where they found me."

"No, we're going to a different one, Alhambra Hospital not far from East Los Angeles." He glanced at her. "How are you feeling?"

"Better now." She managed a smile, but then her eyes filled with tears again. "I'm so glad you came for me, Nico. I knew you would."

"Always." He frowned, noticing the bruise on her cheek and the smear of blood staining the front of her white nightgown. His gut clenched with anger and fear. "What happened? Who hit you?"

She turned away. "Simon, but it doesn't matter. I'm fine."

He sincerely doubted it and wanted to punch Simon for assaulting her. A wave of fury clouded his vision, but he pushed it off with an effort. They weren't completely out of danger yet, they needed to get Ava to the hospital.

Without any Death Rays members following them.

He caught Hudd's grim glance in the rearview mirror. He could tell Hudd was thinking the same thing he was.

What sort of pathetic excuse of a man would hit a pregnant woman? Especially a woman carrying his child?

Nico's fingers tightened on the steering wheel, wishing he could wrap them around Simon's throat. He had to work hard to remain calm, knowing it was best for Ava and her baby.

And now that he had Ava and Callie safe, he wasn't going to let Simon or his Death Rays buddies touch either of them ever again.

———

"AVA, meet Hudson. Hudd, this is Jaydon's sister, Ava. You remember her from the funeral."

"I do," Hudd said with a nod.

"Hi." Ava forced a smile, although her emotions were all over the place. Relief at being rescued, horrified that Nico and his fellow SEAL friends had all put themselves in danger, and fear that Simon would still find a way to track her down.

She knew she'd never be safe. Not as long as Simon was alive. He'd made it clear he intended to seek revenge. And that he still had those pictures that portrayed her stabbing Banjo in the neck, seemingly without provocation.

Knowing Simon, he had retained the entire video feed.

"I'm glad to see you again," she managed.

"Ditto," Hudd said, reaching up to awkwardly pat Ava's shoulder. "We're all glad you're safe."

"Even though my being here is my own fault?" Ava battled a wave of self-loathing. For the millionth time, she wished she hadn't been so stupid and naïve to have fallen for Simon's fake charm.

"We've done that and more for those less deserving," Hudd responded. "Personally, I find it much easier to put myself in a tough situation to help a woman I know and respect."

Hudd didn't know her, not really, but she knew what he meant. Like Nico, Hudd would do whatever was necessary for Jaydon's sister.

Tears slipped down her cheeks. She quickly swiped at them, hoping the guys wouldn't notice.

Stupid hormones.

"Hey, I told you before, everyone makes mistakes," Nico said. "You deserve to be safe, Ava. And so does your baby."

He was right about the baby. She wasn't sure how she'd managed to fall asleep while being locked inside the warehouse. One minute she was doing deep breathing and relaxation exercises to bring her blood pressure down, the next Nico was there.

The way he'd placed his hand over her mouth had scared her to death, and she'd kicked out in a weak effort to get free. But only for a moment. Nico's unique scent had quickly reassured her, as did his husky voice in her ear.

"Are you sure you're feeling okay?" Nico kept shooting concerned glances her way. "No headaches or nausea?"

"I'm fine." She decided not to mention the symptoms she'd experienced earlier. They weren't bothering her now, which she hoped was a good sign.

Nico touched his earpiece for a moment, his expression turning grim. "Thanks, Kaleb, see if you can lose them before you get to the hospital. Mason's injury can be assessed once we get there."

"Mason's injury?" Ava reached out to grab Nico's arm. "What happened to Mason?"

"Knife wound, he claims it's nothing serious." Nico didn't smile, though, which she knew meant he was worried about Mason's injury too. "And no one else was hurt as far as I know." Nico glanced at the rearview. "Unless you're holding back on me too?"

"Nah, I'm fine," Hudson said with a wave of his hand. "I take it one of the other vehicles has a Death Ray on their tail?"

"Yeah. Two motorcycles are on Kaleb's six. But I'm sure he'll lose them in time to get Mason to the hospital."

"What about Bryce and Callie?" Hudd asked.

"They're good. Seems the Death Rays decided against following a police K9 vehicle," Nico said dryly.

Ava swallowed hard, sending up a silent prayer that Mason's injury wasn't too serious. "Have you seen Callie? Is she okay?"

"Bryce got her out safely, they were behind us the entire time." Nico frowned. "You didn't see her once you were at the warehouse?"

"No. I was put in the room and locked in." She shivered, suddenly chilled. "Simon might have still been there if not for some delayed shipment that required his attention."

"Delayed shipment of what?" Nico asked.

"I don't know." She could feel herself getting tense and smoothed her hands over her stomach to relax. "I didn't ask."

Again, Nico seemed to exchange a knowing look with Hudd.

"Ava, how did Simon's guy get to you?" Nico asked. "You were on the locked OB unit, right? Did the Death Rays somehow get past the security on that floor?"

"No, the problem is that I went down to the cafeteria," she admitted. Stupid tears welled in her eyes again. "I thought I was safe or I never would have left. I was thinking of getting something to eat out of the vending machines when the guy came up behind me. He had a gun and told me he'd kill me and the single security guard sitting at the front desk if I didn't go with him."

"Hey, it's okay. Don't cry." Nico looked somewhat panicked. "I don't blame you, Ava."

"Why not? If I wouldn't have left the stupid floor, none of this would have happened!"

"That's not true. They may have tried to get you no matter where you were. My plan all along was to call in the team to get Callie," Nico said firmly. "Besides, it's my fault you were found at the hospital. Those kids we ran into were lookouts for Simon's biker gang."

"They were?" She gaped at him in shock. That possibility had never crossed her mind.

"I heard Simon say something about having sources and knowing where to find you," Nico said. "Unfortunately, I wasn't in a position where I could get away from the warehouse quickly. Not without triggering the cameras. I was ten minutes too late. I returned just in time to see you being put in a car and driven away."

"I thought that was you," she admitted. "I hoped and prayed you'd find me."

"It took longer than I thought to get the team together and for us to sneak up to the building, taking care of the guards on duty." Nico reached over to take her hand. "I knew the success of our mission depended on getting in and out as quietly as possible. Thanks for doing your part."

She understood better now that she'd learned about the motion cameras. Moving with extreme slowness had been one of the hardest things she'd ever done. And Nico had his entire team facing that threat getting in and out of the warehouse. "I owe you my life, Nico."

"No, you don't owe me anything." His voice was uncharacteristically sharp. But then he softened. "I care about you, Ava. I don't need your gratitude. I just want to make sure you and Jaydon or Jayne are okay."

"Jaydon or Jayne, huh?" Hudd echoed. A smile creased his scarred face. "I like those names. And I think Jaydon would be honored to have a son named after him."

Ava smiled. "He would, but I think I'm having a girl."

"That's okay too," Hudd said with a shrug. "Jaydon would still be proud of you, Ava. And he wouldn't want you beating yourself up for making a few mistakes. None of us are perfect, only God has that privilege. Where would we all be if God didn't forgive our sins?"

"You're right, Hudson. Thank you." She did her best to let it go, although the painful bruise on her cheek was a niggling reminder of her foolishness.

The night sky was still dark when Nico pulled into the parking lot of a hospital, bigger than the one she was in before. It worried her that Nico would have to pay for her to be seen again, but she tried to let that guilt go too.

Wallowing in guilt wouldn't change her current situation, not for the better. It could, however, potentially harm her baby.

*No stress*, she repeated. She took a deep breath and let it out slowly. *No stress.*

Nico pulled right up to the front door of the ER. He quickly helped her out, then took Zulu out of the back hatch. Hudd slid out, and Nico tossed him the keys. "Park it for me, would you?"

"Sure." Hudd didn't waste any time getting behind the wheel.

Nico put his arm around her waist as they walked inside. When he spied a wheelchair, he grabbed it. She swallowed a groan and took a seat, knowing it was for the best.

The only good thing about showing up at four thirty in the morning was that there weren't many people in the waiting room.

Ava filled in the triage nurse on her situation. She focused only on the preeclampsia, not the whole being kidnapped at gunpoint thing. The nurse eyed the bruise on her face warily, then stared pointedly at Nico. "Did you hit her?"

"No! He saved me from the man who hit me," Ava hastened to reassure her. "The baby's father, Simon, hit me. Nico is the one who took me away from him."

The nurse didn't look completely convinced as she began taking her blood pressure. Ava mustered all the calmness she possessed to ensure her blood pressure was as low as possible.

"Not bad, one forty over eighty-two," the nurse said.

Ava sent up a silent prayer of relief. "I'm glad it's not too high."

"I'll have the doctor check you out, but it seems to me that you don't need to be admitted to the hospital. I see you don't have insurance, and honestly, we're short on open beds anyway. If your symptoms are under control, we'll probably send you home to rest."

Send her home? Ava had to blink away more tears.

She didn't have a home.

# CHAPTER TEN

It had never occurred to Nico that the hospital staff wouldn't admit Ava. Even when he'd offered to pay out of pocket, the doc on duty informed them it wasn't necessary. In the doc's opinion, Ava could rest anywhere, she didn't have to stay in the hospital unless something changed.

"I wish I had something other than a nightgown to wear," Ava whispered as they headed back to the waiting room.

"You look fine, and we'll stop and grab some new things as soon as we can." To his eye, the nightgown didn't look that much different from her sundresses, but he would get more maternity clothes for her anyway. She deserved to be comfortable.

As he and Ava returned to the waiting room, he saw Hudd waiting there with Zulu. "Have you heard from the others?" he asked, taking Zulu's leash. "I thought Mason would meet us here to have his injury assessed."

"Mason doesn't want to come in for medical care, he's concerned about the doc reporting the wound to the police." Hudd shrugged. "He's right about that."

"Yeah, okay." Nico dragged his hand through his dark hair. "Did they shake the bikers loose from their tail?"

"They did." Hudd glanced at Ava. "She's not staying?"

"Nope. The doc claims there's no reason to admit her for further observation." Nico wondered if the response would have been different if they'd headed back to the original hospital, but going there was too big of a risk. He had no doubt there was a biker stationed someplace nearby watching the place. Seems Simon had bikers and watchers everywhere. "Where are Bryce and Callie?"

"Waiting to hear the plan." A slight smile kicked up the corner of Hudd's mouth. "Callie is demanding to see for herself that Ava is okay."

"Oh, please let me talk to her," Ava said. "I'm sure she's been terrified since being taken from the Lizard Lounge at gunpoint."

Hudd lifted a brow, clearly curious about the Lizard Lounge, but simply held out his phone to Ava. "Call Bryce, he'll be glad to have you speak with Callie."

"Bryce?" Ava asked as she took the phone. "I'm sorry, I don't remember him."

"He's a K9 cop working here in LA, but he also was a SEAL. He was discharged from active duty several years ago."

Ava nodded and looked uncertainly at the phone. Nico was about to help her when she pressed the button and lifted the device to her ear.

"Hi, Bryce? This is Ava. May I speak with Callie?"

Nico assumed Bryce handed the phone over because Ava sank into a seat, her expression one of relief.

"Oh, Callie, I'm so glad you're okay. Yes, I'm fine, and so is the baby." More silence as Ava listened, then she said, "I'm not sure what the plan is. We'll have to trust these men to protect us from Simon and the other Death Rays. Try to hang in there, we'll be together soon, okay?" She disconnected from the call and handed Hudd his phone. "Thank you. It helped for me to hear Callie's voice."

"Let's get out of here," Nico said. "We'll have a conference call with the others to figure out our next steps."

"Sounds good," Hudd agreed.

Nico took Ava's hand, following as Hudd led the way outside to the spot where he'd parked the SUV. Dawn was brightening the sky now, and the adrenaline rush that had hit hard during the infiltration of the warehouse was fading fast.

"We need to find some place to eat breakfast." Nico slid in behind the wheel, glancing at Ava. "I'm sure you're hungry."

"I am, yes," she agreed.

"Okay, find a restaurant and I'll have the rest of the team meet us there." Hudd held up his phone.

"Bryce and Callie too?" Ava asked.

"Of course. They're part of the team now." Nico had been impressed with Bryce's stealth as they'd infiltrated the warehouse. The guy had done well, not to mention he'd been incredibly silent behind him.

"Yep," Hudd said.

Ava seemed relieved to hear that, making him realize it might be a relief for Ava to have another woman with her. Especially now that he'd brought his entire SEAL team to Los Angeles. Talk about a testosterone overload.

"Hudd, use that phone to find a breakfast place, would you?" Nico concentrated on driving through the already congested traffic. "The closer the better."

"Found one." Hudd gave Nico brief directions to the

place, then called the others to inform them of the location. "We're set. We'll need a table for nine."

"And three dogs," Ava added.

"Yeah. Too bad we all weren't able to bring our K9s with us," Hudd said.

"I know, sorry about that." Nico met Hudd's gaze in the rearview mirror. "I didn't have time to ask how Kendra was doing."

A smile lit up Hudd's features. "She's great. And she's expecting too."

"Hey, congrats, man!" That was welcome news to hear. Nico had heard that Kendra had lost a child several years ago to cancer. He was glad they were starting a new family together.

"Thanks." Normally Hudd wasn't much of a talker, but being married to Kendra had mellowed the guy. "We're excited."

"With good reason." Nico glanced at Ava who was smoothing her hands over her stomach. "Are you feeling okay?"

"Yes, and you don't have to keep asking me that." Ava managed a small smile. "I'll tell you if I'm not feeling well."

"Promise?" He knew he was being overprotective, but he couldn't help it. Her pregnancy was complicated by preeclampsia, which was serious, no matter how mild the doc claimed it was. He intended to know the moment she wasn't feeling well so they could get back to the emergency department.

Maybe a different hospital this time as he hadn't been thrilled with the care Ava had received at the last one.

The good news was that all the hospitals shared the same electronic medical record, so at least they'd be able to see what had transpired at her previous visits. Which now that he thought about it may have contributed to why they hadn't admitted her to be observed for twenty-four hours.

He inwardly winced, realizing that the way Ava had disappeared from the hospital in the middle of the night probably didn't look good for her. The medical staff didn't know that she'd been forced to leave.

Whatever. There would be time to set the record straight soon enough. For now, they needed food and a place to stay. In that order.

He pulled into the parking lot of the restaurant ten minutes later. The dining room wasn't too busy, which was good since they needed several tables pushed together to accommodate the entire group.

Kaleb, Mason, Dallas, and Dawson arrived next. Nico eyed Mason curiously, but if his buddy was in pain from his injury, he didn't show it. "Everything okay?"

"Peachy," Mason said. "I'm fine."

"We stopped at a drug store and cleaned up his wound," Dallas added. "Thankfully, it wasn't as bad as I'd originally feared."

"Glad to hear it." Nico knew God had watched over them on their mission. To have escaped relatively unscathed was nothing short of a miracle.

Their server was busy bringing coffee and water for the table.

"Decaf for me, please," Ava said with a weary smile.

He reached over to squeeze her hand. Based on what little sleep she'd gotten, he could sympathize with her disappointment over sticking with decaf. Yet he also knew Ava wouldn't do anything to harm her baby. And caffeine probably wasn't good as far as keeping her blood pressure under control either.

"Are you ready to order?" their server asked.

"We're waiting on two more people." The moment Nico said the words, he saw Bryce and Callie enter the restaurant. "They're here now, maybe give them a few minutes to check out the menu?"

"Of course." The server moved away.

"Ava!" Callie broke away from Bryce to rush toward the table. Ava stood, and the two women clung to each other for a long moment. "I was so worried about you and the baby," Callie whispered.

"I was worried about you too." Ava's eyes were bright with tears. "We're safe now, Callie."

"I know." Callie stepped back and looked at the table of men who'd all jumped to their feet when Ava and Callie had embraced. She seemed taken aback but managed to smile and nod. "I need to thank all of you for helping us escape."

"No thanks are necessary," Mason said firmly. "This is the least we could do. And I speak for all of us when I say we're glad you're both safe."

Callie still looked uncertain, so he quickly made another round of introductions. There hadn't been time for that when they'd rushed from the warehouse.

"I hope there isn't a test," Callie joked.

"Nope. We answer to just about anything, don't we, guys?" Mason teased.

Callie took a seat beside Ava, leaving Bryce to take the last seat on the other side of the table. He had Kirby on leash at his side, and they'd instinctively put some distance between each of the K9s.

Nico figured Zulu was just happy to be out of the SUV for a while. He'd need to spend some time with her soon. She deserved a reward for her good behavior.

Their server returned and took their breakfast orders. Then she refilled coffee cups and water glasses.

"We need to find a place to stay," Nico said, interrupting the small talk. "Ava needs to rest and relax."

"I'll see if I can find a property that has several bedrooms," Kaleb offered. "I'm sure there's something nearby."

"What's the plan moving forward?" Mason asked.

"Good question." Nico sighed and scrubbed a hand over his face. "We need to figure out how to eliminate Simon as a threat. He had his biker buddies take both women at gunpoint, so we have to assume he'll try again."

"I'm curious about what was in those boxes at the warehouse," Dawson drawled. Since he'd returned to live in Montana, his cowboy accent had grown even more pronounced. "Seems like uncovering whatever criminal activity he's involved with is the fastest way to get him and the others behind bars."

"True," Dallas agreed.

The rest of the team nodded, including Bryce.

"He mentioned a problem with a shipment." Ava unconsciously fingered the bruise darkening her cheek. "That's why he left me alone in the room."

"Callie, do you know anything?" Bryce asked.

"No, why would I?" she shot back. It seemed as if the two hadn't hit it off very well during their brief time together.

"I'm not insinuating anything, I just thought maybe you'd overheard something too," Bryce said with a frown.

"Abe is the man who took me from the hospital," Ava said, drawing the attention back to her. "Apparently, he's Banjo's brother."

"And who is Banjo?" Hudd asked.

Ava flushed and stared down at the table for a minute before meeting Hudd's gaze. "He's the man I killed while escaping Simon the first time."

The table fell into shocked silence for a moment. Then Mason said, "I'm sorry you had to do that, Ava, but I'm glad you did what was necessary to get away."

"Hear, hear," Kaleb echoed. "Strong women rock."

Nico smiled as Ava looked surprised by the compliment. Bryce raised a brow, but Nico gave him a small shake of his head. He'd fill Bryce in on the details later.

This was a time to be thankful for what they had survived and accomplished.

When their server returned with their meals, Nico's teammates looked instinctively to Kaleb to say grace. But Nico quickly spoke up. "My turn," he said, taking Ava's hand. "Dear Lord, we are eternally grateful for the protection You provided for us earlier today. We ask for Your guidance as we continue to seek justice for those who have harmed others. And we thank You for this wonderful food. Amen."

"Amen," the others chorused. Even Bryce had participated, while Callie looked surprised by the prayer.

The first phase of their mission was a success, but the danger was far from over. And Nico wouldn't rest until Simon was no longer a threat to Ava or Callie.

And looking at his teammates around the table, he knew they wouldn't leave until the job was done either.

---

AVA SMILED REASSURINGLY at Callie who seemed intimidated by all the men seated around the table. "It's going to be okay," she whispered.

"Are you sure about that?" Callie spoke in a low voice too. "I can't believe your friends brought a cop in to rescue us."

Ava knew Callie didn't trust cops as far as she could throw them. Which, considering her small size, wasn't very far. "Dallas is a cop, too, but you can see right now they only care about our safety. That's all that matters."

"Yeah, maybe." Callie dug in to her breakfast. "Yum. This is great. I'm so hungry. Simon didn't give me anything to eat while I was stuck in that room."

Ava frowned. "That's unusual, even for him."

Callie shrugged. "He made it clear I was being punished."

Ava knew Simon held grudges for longer than any normal person should. Like continuing to come after her because she'd killed Banjo.

She was hungry too. That stupid decision she'd made to go down to the vending machines still haunted her. Zulu reached her head up to nudge her hand, and she petted the Doberman's sleek fur.

No one would ever guess there were three dogs at this table. They were incredibly well behaved.

"Don't you have to feed Zulu?" she asked.

Nico nodded. "As soon as we get settled somewhere. I didn't think bringing a bowl of her kibble into the restaurant would be smart," he added wryly.

She smiled, then winced as her cheek throbbed. She considered using her water glass as an ice pack, but she knew if she did that, Nico would insist on getting her a real one. No need to distract him from more important matters.

The time she'd spent locked in Simon's warehouse already seemed like a long time ago. She wanted to ask if the guys had killed any of Simon's men, but she didn't want to sound bloodthirsty. She assumed they hadn't used any more force than was necessary.

They were honorable men. Men of faith and courage. Not a single one had balked at coming to help get her and Callie away from the Death Rays.

She placed a hand over her belly, realizing she and her baby were only alive because of Nico and his SEAL teammates.

And she had God to thank for sending each and every one of them.

Feeling Nico's concerned gaze, she went back to finishing her meal. It seemed the entire group was hungry as the talking slowed to a minimum.

When they were finished, Kaleb went to work on his phone. It wasn't long before he announced, "I found a place."

"How far away?" Nico asked.

Kaleb flashed a grin. "Fifteen minutes without traffic, your guess is as good as mine at this hour of the day."

Nico groaned but nodded. "That's fine, thanks." He gestured for the bill, and the guys around the table began tossing money at him. It hit Ava that Jaydon would have been right at home with these men. He would have done the same thing, even if he was asked to rescue some woman he didn't know.

"I've got this," Nico said. But, of course, none of the men took their money back.

Callie watched the men interact with a bemused expression too. Ava impulsively took her hand. "Completely different from the Death Rays, huh?"

"You got that right," Callie murmured. "I'm trying to figure out if they're for real or if this is a big act for our benefit?"

"It's for real," Ava assured her. "They are an impressive bunch."

"Except for Bryce Flynn," Callie said. "I still don't trust him."

Ava frowned. "Did he say or do something concerning?"

"No, nothing like that," Callie hastened to reassure her. "He's just a cop. And he looked concerned when you mentioned killing Banjo."

Yeah, Ava had noticed that too. But she tried not to stress about it. Especially now when stress was the enemy to her child.

Besides, she felt certain Nico wouldn't let her go to jail. A fear she'd lived with for months now. Ever since the glossy photos had appeared under the door of her decrepit motel room.

Unfortunately, Simon still had copies of the photos along with the video of the entire incident. The very thought of a cop or worse, a prosecutor, watching the way she'd stabbed Banjo made her shiver.

"Everyone ready to go?" Nico asked.

A chorus of yeses rippled around the table. Ava didn't hear anything from Callie, so she glanced over. "Ready?"

Callie shrugged and nodded. "Why not?"

Ava was concerned about her younger friend. She was worried Callie wouldn't hang around for long with Bryce in the group. She knew Callie had a criminal record for drug use, although she'd been clean for as long as Ava had known her. Ava suspected there were other things that Callie may have done in her past that made her leery of law enforcement too.

Nico slipped his arm beneath her elbow to help her stand. She flashed him a grateful smile, desperately wishing she was wearing something other than her nightgown. Not that any of the restaurant patrons had seemed to notice.

Her bruised cheek had gotten some looks and the fact that she was pregnant. She told herself these strangers didn't matter, but it bothered her that they thought Nico had done this to her.

Nothing could be further from the truth.

"I'm driving with you," Callie whispered, sticking close to her side.

"That's fine," she assured her. Then leaned toward Nico to say, "Callie is riding with us."

Nico nodded and shot a knowing glance toward Bryce. The K9 cop appeared to understand the change in riding arrangements, heading toward his SUV, Kirby at his side, without comment.

Hudd turned his head toward them, then lightly jogged toward Bryce. "Okay if I bum a ride?"

"Sure." Bryce opened the back hatch for Kirby. "I'd like company."

"Meet you there," Nico called.

The ride should have been fifteen minutes but would no doubt take much longer in the bumper-to-bumper traffic. Callie closed her eyes and rested during the ride, so Ava did the same. Having a full stomach helped her feel better, although she was still plagued by fatigue.

The lack of having a headache or nausea was also a good sign.

Nico held her hand during the entire ride. She told herself he was offering moral support considering her diagnosis, but she couldn't deny the tingle of awareness rippling up her arm at his touch.

"Where do you shop for maternity clothes?" Nico asked, breaking the silence.

"A discount store works fine." She glanced at the passing street signs to get her bearings. "I think there's one coming up on the right."

"We'll make a quick stop there so you can get what you need." He glanced in the rearview mirror. "Callie can pick up some things too."

"I wouldn't mind getting out of this dumb uniform," Callie said wryly. She was still wearing the Lizard Lounge serving outfit. "I don't normally dress like this."

"I'm sure you don't," Nico said reassuringly. "And don't worry, everything you want to buy is on me."

Ava wanted to protest, Nico had done nothing but spend money on her, but she wasn't sure how much cash Callie had, so she didn't argue. She didn't want to put her friend in an awkward position.

As if Callie wasn't uncomfortable enough already.

Ava knew these men at least peripherally. Nico had come around the most during breaks between deployments, but she'd met the others too.

Callie was getting a megadose of SEALs today.

The side trip to the discount store didn't take long. Ava picked out three maternity dresses and some underclothes, while Callie picked out shorts and T-shirts, her usual ensemble. Nico had given Ava his credit card, giving them privacy to get the things they needed while keeping an eye on them from afar with Zulu at his side.

Ava was tempted to change her clothes in the store but decided to wait until she could freshen up with a shower.

"All set?" Nico asked as they joined him.

"Yes, thanks." She gave him his credit card back. "We appreciate your generosity."

"Anytime." Nico pushed the door open so they could return to the SUV.

The sun was high enough to warm the temperature. Callie lifted her face to the sun as if appreciating being outside.

They piled back into the SUV. Nico threaded the vehicle back into traffic. "We should be at the house in the next twenty minutes or so."

"Good. I plan to toss this stupid uniform in the garbage. After I take a long, hot shower," Callie said.

"I'm with you," Ava agreed.

Nico took her hand again. She glanced at him curiously, but he simply smiled at her as if their holding hands was entirely natural.

It made her think about their sizzling and all too brief kiss.

She'd been telling herself for the past two days that her hormones were out of control from her pregnancy, but glancing at Nico, she silently acknowledged she was lying to herself. She cared for Nico far more than she should.

If she wasn't careful, the handsome SEAL would break her heart.

# CHAPTER ELEVEN

The rental house Kaleb had found wasn't as bad as he'd feared. By the time Nico and the women had arrived, the SEAL team had walked the perimeter and were already discussing guard duty and safety strategies.

"Two of the three bedrooms are for the women," Mason said, automatically stepping back into a leadership role. "Anyone taking naps during the day can use the third bedroom. If we're all here, we'll mostly bunk on the living room floor with the dogs."

"Do we get to flip a coin for the sofa?" Dawson asked with a grin.

"We'll rotate that position, along with the bedroom depending on how long we end up staying here." Mason turned toward Nico. "We need to discuss our next steps related to Simon and the Death Rays."

"And we should consider getting other cops involved," Bryce said. "I was on board with using your team to get the women out safely, but now that they are, we need to notify my boss and the gang unit."

Nico hesitated, then glanced over his shoulder to make sure the women were out of earshot. Both Callie and Ava had been anxious to shower and change into fresh clothes. He doubted it would take that long. "Here's the problem. Simon has incriminating photographs and video of Ava stabbing a guy named Banjo. She did it to get away after Simon abused her and tried to strangle her. She didn't intend to kill him, but upon stabbing him in the neck, she accidentally hit his carotid artery. He then bled to death. Ava had gone to a shelter, but then when she saw one of the Death Rays outside, she took off from there too. Bottom line, Ava is scared she'll end up having her baby in jail. I saw the photos, they don't look good for her. We would be able to prove the abuse, but that was from Simon not this guy Banjo." Nico swept his gaze over the group. "Ava has also been diagnosed with a mild form of preeclampsia. The doc made it clear she's to stay off her feet and avoid stress. I don't think jail will help, it will only add an additional risk to her and the baby."

There was a long moment of silence as the group of men digested that information.

"Okay, no cops," Kaleb was quick to agree. "Ava ending up in jail isn't an option."

"Works for me," Dawson said.

"You know, there are two cops here already." Dallas glanced at Bryce, who looked surprised. "Fredericksburg PD in Texas."

"Yeah, but you're both off the clock, right?" Mason asked.

Nico waited until Bryce reluctantly nodded. "Yeah, okay. No cops yet."

Mason turned toward Nico. "Does she still have copies of the photos?"

"Doubtful, her backpack was in the hospital room when Simon's biker goon took her at gunpoint." Nico settled his gaze on Bryce. "You can see why Ava didn't want you or any other police officers involved."

Bryce sighed and nodded. "Is that why Callie hates cops too?"

"I'm sure Ava's situation is part of the reason, but it sounds like Callie might have a criminal history of her own that makes her leery of the police." Nico shrugged. "At least, that's the impression I got when Ava and Callie were whispering at breakfast."

"I agree on no jail for Ava. To do that, we'll need to find proof that Simon is involved in illegal activities," Hudd said. "Once he's arrested for that, Ava shouldn't have anything to worry about."

"Maybe nothing to worry about." It was a good plan, although he knew they'd also need to find the photos and video in order to make sure they couldn't be used against Ava in a court of law. Simon behind bars wasn't good enough, he'd get a lawyer and likely would try to use the photos and video against Ava, despite being under arrest.

"We start with the crates in the storage warehouse," Nico said, thinking back to the boxes he'd seen stored inside. "If they haven't moved them already."

"If Simon is involved in an ongoing criminal enterprise, he won't be able to get rid of the goods that easily. However, the bikers will be on high alert after losing their hostages." Mason spread his hands wide. "I'm not saying that we don't get what we need, just pointing out the obstacles."

"Understood," Nico agreed. It was part of their training to understand all the potential ways an op could go sideways. Like their last official op for the Navy. "We have a long day ahead of us, but it seems prudent to wait until nighttime to go back inside."

"Inside where?" Ava came toward him, looking amazing in another of her maternity sundresses. He preferred her natural auburn hair, but the blond curls were cute too. His chest tightened when he saw her, and he momentarily forgot what they were talking about. Ava frowned. "Nico? Go where?"

Oh yeah, the warehouse. "We'd like to search for evidence that would incriminate Simon. You mentioned trouble with a shipment, so he's either dealing drugs or guns."

Ava swept her gaze over the SEALs, then lowered her voice. "Um, can we talk for a moment? In private?"

"Sure." Nico moved away from the group and took her arm. "You should be resting," he said in a low voice.

"I'm fine." She dropped into a kitchen chair, then gestured for him to do the same. He sat, eyeing her warily. "I don't want you and the other guys to go back to confront Simon. I think it's best if I just disappear."

What? He stared at her, certain he must have misunderstood. "No. That's not an option."

"I was always planning to head to Mexico after the baby was born," she said, avoiding his gaze. "The sooner I can disappear where Simon can't find me, the better for everyone involved. Callie can come with me, that way we'll both be safe."

He did his best not to show his shocked reaction to her plan to leave the country. "Ava, you can't go back on the run. Not in your current condition." Not ever, as far as he was concerned, but he forced himself to remain calm. "The guys are on board with eliminating Simon as a threat. Not killing him," he hastily amended when her eyes widened.

"But by obtaining the evidence we need to put him behind bars for a long time."

"Nico . . ." She sighed and smoothed her hands over her stomach as if striving to remain calm. "I know you're trying to help, but I'll never feel safe as long as Simon has those photos and video of Banjo's death. His being in prison doesn't change what I've done."

"I know, and I want you to trust me that we'll find that evidence and destroy it." He wanted to take her hands, but she was still rubbing her stomach. "Ava, please. We were able to get you and Callie out without any trouble."

"Mason's injury could have been serious," she quickly interrupted.

"Yes, but it wasn't. Because we're well trained. I need you to give me a few days, Ava. We have a whole team of highly skilled men here. I'm confident we'll get the incriminating video and photos from Simon."

She hesitated, then lowered her head. "Am I a bad person, Nico?" Her voice dropped so low he could barely hear her. "Maybe I should come forward to take accountability for what I've done."

"You are absolutely not a bad person. You only did what was necessary to save your life, Ava." He couldn't stop himself from reaching for her hands now and holding them against his chest. "There isn't a man here who believes you belong in jail. If you hadn't stabbed Banjo, you might not be sitting here today."

"I want to believe that." She closed her eyes, tears slipping down her cheeks. "I didn't want to kill him. I only wanted to get away. But he would have kept me there against my will." She blinked, then lifted her head. "I know he would have taken me right back to Simon."

Nico wasn't a lawyer, but he could guess what the next

question from a defense attorney might be. "Did you think that because Banjo had done that in the past?"

"Not Banjo, but another of the Death Rays did." She pulled her hand away to wipe at her face. "It was common knowledge that Simon wanted me to stay with him, no matter what. They constantly watched me."

He'd hoped it was Banjo specifically who had prevented her from leaving. That Banjo was the one who'd held her at the warehouse against her will, taking her by force back over to Simon. It would have helped her claim of self-defense.

Yet he didn't doubt her side of the story. He knew Ava wouldn't have stabbed anyone unless she truly feared for her life. And catching Banjo off guard was the only way to overpower the guy. All the bikers he'd seen were easily twice Ava's size.

And there were also Simon's actions after the fact to take into consideration. First following her from one place to the next, including the women's shelter, then sending someone to kidnap her from the hospital at gunpoint. All important factors that added credence to her story.

"Ava, please. Please give me and the rest of the guys some time to come up with a plan of action." He smiled encouragingly. "God brought all of us here for a reason. We'll find a way to get the video and photos back. And once we have those, you and your baby will be safe no matter where you choose to live." Hopefully that wouldn't be in Mexico, although he kept that thought to himself.

She was quiet for so long he feared she was attempting to come up with additional arguments. Then she nodded. "Okay, fine. But I don't want anyone to be hurt because of me." She lifted her head, anguish in her eyes. "I feel bad enough about killing Banjo. I don't think I could live with myself if one of Jaydon's teammates or Bryce became seriously injured over this plan of yours."

A large weight fell from Nico's shoulders. Yet he didn't take her concerns lightly. Every time they'd gone on an op, they'd done so knowing they were risking their lives for their country.

This would be no different. And truthfully? He worried about the guys too. They had wives and children now.

"Thank you for believing in us, Ava. I want you to know we'll do everything possible to get what we need without putting ourselves in harm's way." He was speaking mostly on behalf of the rest of the guys.

Nico knew that he'd gladly risk his life to make sure Ava was free from Simon's clutches once and for all.

---

AVA DIDN'T LIKE the idea of Nico and the others heading back to Simon's warehouse. Especially not for her sake.

If not for the stupid video and photographs, these guys could all head home and turn Simon's activities over to the police.

Although she couldn't quite figure out why the police hadn't arrested Simon and his men before now. She'd stayed out of his business ventures, but now she wished she'd paid closer attention.

"I wish there was something I could do to help." Resigned to the plan, she met Nico's gaze. "I don't know what is in those crates, but I believe Simon received shipments on a regular basis."

Nico's eyebrows lifted. "A regular schedule?"

"Yes. Tuesday, Thursday, and Saturday nights." She frowned. With everything that had happened, she'd completely lost track of the days. "If there was a shipment last night, which was Tuesday, right? Then there won't be another shipment until Thursday night."

"Unless the trouble with the shipment put them off schedule." Nico's dark gaze turned thoughtful. "Could be that the shipment was delayed and will actually be coming in tonight."

"Maybe." She almost hoped not, one night of peace and quiet wasn't too much to ask. "Either way, he has guys going to the ocean to pick up whatever is coming in." She hesitated, then said, "I've always thought it was drugs, but I never asked." She grimaced. "I guess I didn't really want to know."

"That's fine, I'm glad you don't know specific details of Simon's enterprise." Nico's tone was reassuring. "Better for you in the long run. And I'm sure we'll know soon enough once we get a peek inside those crates."

Maybe, but that didn't change the fact that she'd been a foolish, naïve, coward. She'd believed Simon to be a bad-boy member of a motorcycle club without realizing the club needed to have financing. What kind of idiot believes any of those bikers worked real, legitimate jobs for a living?

"How many men did he send to get the shipments?" Nico asked. "I'm sure they didn't bring those crates to the warehouse on the back of a motorcycle."

"No, they used a panel van." She thought back for a moment. "The same van they used to kidnap me. Simon sent two guys in the van, but several others would accompany them on their bikes."

Nico nodded thoughtfully. "Okay, that helps. You don't

know where they get these shipments, do you? Like what dock or pier?"

"Pier thirteen," another female voice said. Ava glanced over Nico's shoulder to see Callie standing there. She'd showered and changed into her usual attire, leaving her short, dark hair to dry naturally.

"How do you know that?" Nico asked, shifting his chair to include Callie in the conversation.

"Otto told me." Callie shrugged. "He talked a lot when he drank, which was pretty often."

"Did Simon know that Otto talked to you?" Ava was worried about Callie now more than ever. "Is that why Simon came after you at the Lizard Lounge?"

"Nah, he only came after me to get to you," Callie said without hesitation. "He figured you'd try to find me, and you did." She grinned. "Although not in the way Simon expected."

Ava noticed that Bryce edged closer to hear the conversation. Callie didn't bother to look at him. "I hope not," Nico drawled.

Callie nodded. "I'm not sure if he knew how much Otto blabbed when he was drunk. Although it shouldn't have been a surprise."

That much was true. Ava knew Simon had his bikers on a tight leash. A situation that had sometimes caused rumblings among the crew. She'd tried to use that discontent to her advantage, but when push came to shove, the bikers were loyal to Simon.

Not to her or Callie.

"Did Otto say anything else?" Nico asked. "Like what sort of boats were coming in?"

Callie frowned, her expression thoughtful. "I don't know that Otto ever mentioned the types of boats he was going to meet, but I got the impression they were smaller, personal boats. Not larger ones. I seem to remember him saying something about sneaking into the slip without being noticed."

"Interesting," Nico murmured.

"Was Otto your boyfriend?" Bryce asked.

Callie narrowed her gaze. "That's not any of your business. I'm not a part of the Death Rays anymore and couldn't care less if every last one of them ends up in jail." Without saying anything more, she spun on her heel and walked away.

Ava glanced at Nico who shrugged and looked over at Bryce.

"What? It was a simple question," Bryce protested.

"Not really." Ava lifted her chin. "Just because Callie and I were foolish enough to get involved with these guys doesn't mean we're criminals too. Don't judge us, Bryce."

He winced. "I'm sorry, that wasn't my intent."

"Maybe not, but that's how Callie heard it." Ava reminded herself not to become upset on Callie's behalf. "Can you honestly say you've never made a mistake? That you've never trusted the wrong person?"

"No, I can't claim to be perfect," Bryce said in a low voice. "I've made plenty of mistakes." He glanced toward the hallway leading to the bedrooms. "I'll apologize."

"You may want to wait a bit," Nico advised. "Seems like Callie isn't your biggest fan."

"No lie," Bryce muttered as he turned away. Then he abruptly swung back to face her. "I'm sorry I've hurt you and your friend, Ava."

"It's fine, Bryce. Just know we're both keenly aware of the mistakes we've made that have placed you and the others in danger."

"Like Nico said, we put our lives on the line for strangers every day. Doing so for those you care about is even better." Bryce glanced down at his K9, Kirby. "Time for a bathroom break, huh, buddy?"

Ava couldn't help but smile as Zulu perked up at seeing Kirby. As if the two dogs were already friends because their owners were. "I'll go with you," Nico said, rising to his feet. "I need to give Zulu some play time."

Ava watched them go, then stood as well. She'd given Nico all the information she had about Simon's so-called business. Her rough night was catching up with her, and she desperately wanted to take a nap.

But she paused outside Callie's room first. After lightly knocking at the door, she heard Callie's muffled, "Who is it?"

"Me, Ava." She waited a beat, then entered the room. "Hey, are you okay?"

"Fine." Callie was stretched out on the bed, lying on her stomach in a way Ava hadn't been able to do for months now. It made her yearn for her prepregnancy body in a way she'd never thought possible.

"Hey, don't let Bryce upset you." She sat on the edge of the bed beside Callie. "He didn't mean to judge us."

Callie let out a harsh laugh. "Oh, I think he did. Cops are always looking down on people who might hang out with people who have broken the law. He's just not used to women calling him on his behavior."

Callie had always carried a chip on her shoulder, and Ava had never pushed the woman to discuss their respective pasts. She'd sensed hers had been a cakewalk compared to Callie's, so she'd left it up to the younger woman to decide how much or how little to say. Besides, it was all they could do to eke out a living day to day, barely making ends meet.

"He knows he's not perfect, Callie. And he risked his life to save you."

"That's what cops are supposed to do," Callie said, although the edge had vanished from her tone. She sighed and rolled up on her side. "Listen, I'm not trying to be rude. I'm grateful he and the others got us out of there, Ava. I was convinced Simon would kill me the moment he got his hands on you. I'm sure Bryce is a good cop, it's just that I don't trust cops in general."

"Because a cop hurt you in the past?"

Callie slowly nodded. "Yeah, but I don't want to talk about it. I know there are good cops and bad cops, just like there are good and bad people. It's over and done now." She abruptly changed the subject. "How long are we going to be stuck here anyway?"

"I'm not sure." Ava glanced around the room. "You have to admit it's nicer here than our dumpy apartment. I haven't seen a single creepy-crawly."

Callie reluctantly smiled. "You got that right. No noisy neighbors partying late every night, which is refreshing. And I don't miss the groping guys at the Lizard Lounge either," she agreed.

"Pedro tried to look after us, but he couldn't be everywhere." Pedro was one of the better bosses she'd had over the past few months. "He wasn't like Carlos who was awfully handsy himself. Remember when I twisted his hand behind his back and he squealed like a girl?"

"Yeah." Callie chuckled, then sat up and placed her hand on Ava's stomach. "How's Jaydon doing today?"

"Jayne is fine, thanks," she teased. Despite how she seemed to hate men in general, Callie firmly believed she was having a boy. "At this point, I'm hoping and praying I'll be able to carry this baby to full term."

"Wait, why wouldn't you?" Callie asked.

Ava filled Callie in on her medical problems. "Nothing to worry about, though. I went back to the emergency department this morning, and the doc said I'm doing well enough that I don't need to stay in the hospital. It seems that all I need to do is concentrate on lowering my stress while staying off my feet. As long as I do both of those two things, the baby and I will be just fine."

Callie's frown deepened. "Resting and staying off your feet? That's huge, Ava. It means you can't work. You still have two months to go, don't you?"

"Yes."

"What are we going to do when the danger from Simon is over?" Callie was looking more distressed by the minute. "How are we going to survive?"

It was a good question, one she didn't have an equally good answer to. "I don't know, Callie. The doc was clear that I need to stay off my feet." He'd used the words bed rest, but Ava couldn't imagine lying in bed doing nothing. "We'll figure something out."

Callie didn't say anything for a long moment. "I've seen the way Nico looks at you, Ava. He'll likely support you financially, so you won't have to worry about getting a job. But me? I don't have that luxury. I'll be stuck trying to find a job that will pay me enough to support myself. Rent here in LA is astronomical, at least San Bernardino was slightly better. I'll have to find a new roommate and . . ." Her voice trailed off.

"Nico will help us both, Callie, because that's the kind of guy he is," she said firmly. "Trust me on this."

"I'm not sure about that." Callie turned away, looking more forlorn now than when Ava had first come in to talk to her. "I'd like to get some sleep too. I spent most of my time in the warehouse wide awake. I kept waiting for Simon or Otto to show up and kill me."

"I'm sorry you had to go through that." Ava wanted to continue reassuring Callie that she'd be fine but thought it best to give her some time to digest the change in plan. The two of them had been dependent upon each other for months now, it wouldn't be easy for Callie to accept Nico's help.

Ava wasn't exactly thrilled with the idea either. Yet she didn't have a choice. Working a restaurant job where she was on her feet all day was out of the question.

She would protect her baby, no matter what.

"Talk to you later, Callie." She stood and left Callie alone with her thoughts. Returning to her room, she climbed into bed and rested on her side. It was the only way she could get comfortable these days.

But rest didn't come easily. Her thoughts whirled, especially over Callie's comment. About how Nico looked at her.

Ava hadn't noticed anything out of the ordinary. Nico had always been considerate of her, even when Jaydon was alive. Callie was probably overreacting to Nico's kindness and gentle manner. Callie didn't know Nico was a man of faith. Ava knew that she would always be Jaydon's little sister to Nico and the rest of the guys.

But no, she couldn't take advantage of Nico. She wouldn't force him into being with her out of a sense of duty. An obligation.

She and her baby would find a way to make ends meet. She could maybe go back to being a dental hygienist. After everything she'd been through, a boring life to raise her baby sounded perfect. Back then, most of her days were spent sitting as she cleaned teeth. Even half days might work. She'd make more than being a bartender, that was for sure.

Yes, she had options, and she'd bring Callie along with her. Together they'd figure things out.

The sooner she resigned herself to a future without Nico Ramirez, the better.

# CHAPTER TWELVE

"We need to get eyes on slip number thirteen." Nico glanced at the group of men gathered around him. It was a strange feeling to be in charge of the operation, and he frequently found himself looking at Senior Chief for validation he was on the right track. "I think we could send two teams, one down to the dock, one to the warehouse to find out what's in those crates."

"There are seven of us, we could send a third team to get intel, leaving one guy here to protect the women," Bryce said.

Nico frowned. "I'd rather keep at least two guys here at the house." In truth, he'd rather have most the team remain behind to guard Ava and Callie, but he knew that wasn't logical. There was no way the Desert Death Rays could know where they were staying. "We could send a third guy to the warehouse, if necessary."

"That seems reasonable." Mason gave a thoughtful nod. "I agree with two men staying behind, one covering the back, the other the front."

Bryce looked as if he wanted to argue, but he simply shrugged. "Whatever you think is best."

"What about Simon?" Kaleb asked. "It would be nice to know what he looks like."

"I have a photo of him on a memory card." He pulled the small, flat disk from his pocket, then turned toward the door. "Give me a minute to grab my computer."

It didn't take long for Nico to get the laptop computer booted up and the memory card loaded. The team crowded around him at the kitchen table as he began going through the photos. When the one of Callie chained to the bed popped up, he heard Bryce suck in a harsh breath. He understood how the cop felt, he didn't enjoy seeing a woman kept in chains either. He clicked through and found the grainy photos he'd managed to get of Simon and the guy talking behind the warehouse.

"This is the best shot of Simon." Nico lightly tapped the screen with his index finger. "Long, dark hair pulled back, black leather skullcap, black vest, black jeans, and scar along his cheek."

The entire team stared at the grainy image. Without the flash, it wasn't as clear as he'd hoped, but it was the best he could do under the circumstances.

"Okay, so we know who the bad guy is," Hudd said quietly. "If there's a chance to neutralize him, we should take it."

Nico couldn't disagree but glanced at Bryce. As a cop, he'd be obligated to report a crime. "Getting evidence against him would help keep him neutralized in jail."

Hudd glanced at him without saying anything more. Nico knew Hudd had intended to take Simon out of the picture permanently.

Not outright killing him, engaging him in a fight where

he lost. Maybe not a fair fight, because SEALs were highly trained in combat, but Simon had kidnapped two women, one of them pregnant, and had threatened to kill them both.

Not an empty threat either. Nico knew the biker had fully intended to follow through.

Blowing out a breath, Nico decided to leave Simon's fate in God's hands. They'd do their best to get the evidence they needed to have Simon arrested. But if the guy pulled a gun on any of them, all bets were off.

"Is there anything else we need to do before nightfall?" Mason asked. "Additional gear? My vest helped deflect the biker's knife, which was why the blade only nicked my lower side below the vest."

"Helmets would only make us stand out," Dawson drawled. "So I think our current gear will have to suffice."

"I'd like to take the warehouse," Nico said, changing the thread of the discussion. "I've been there several times already."

"I'll go with you," Kaleb quickly offered.

"I'll take the boat slip," Bryce said. "Callie doesn't like me, so it's better if I'm not the one staying back to offer protection."

"She doesn't like cops in general," Dallas pointed out. "But that's fine, I can take the boat slip with you."

"I'll tag along with Kaleb and Nico." Mason glanced at Dawson and Hudd. "We'll trust you to keep the women safe."

"Okay." Hudd didn't look enthused at being left out of the action, but he seemed to understand the necessity.

Dawson shrugged. "Whatever you need."

Nico managed a smile. "Thanks for coming to help. I couldn't have done this without you."

"It's about time you let us help," Mason countered.

"We've been telling you for months to let us know what we can do to find Ava."

Nico glanced down the hall at the bedrooms. "I'm very glad I found her. And Callie too. They both deserve better than to be hunted like animals by Simon and his biker thugs."

Bryce's expression turned grim, as if remembering the photograph of Callie chained to the bed. "You have that right."

"I'll head out to get some food for lunch and dinner," Mason offered, changing the topic again. "Best we stay here to cook. I'm sure our large group was noticed at breakfast."

"Thanks, Mason." Nico knew it would be difficult for all of them to sit patiently, waiting for nightfall. "We should take turns getting some sleep too. Two guys can bunk down in the spare bedroom on rotation. We need to take turns, as we'll need to be sharp tonight. The Death Rays will be twice as prepared after losing their hostages."

Dallas glanced at Hudd. "Should we take first dibs on sleep?"

"Why not?" The two men stood and made their way to the bedroom. Nico glanced at the clock, then turned back toward Mason.

"Thanks for offering to get food. Grab something simple for lunch, sandwiches are fine. We can use the grill out back for dinner."

"Got it." Mason headed for the door, then paused to look back at Kaleb. "I'll use your SUV, okay?"

"I'll ride with you." Kaleb took his K9, Sierra, outside with him. "We may need to stock up on dog food too."

After the two men left, and the other two men had gone to sleep, the remaining three stayed around the kitchen table. Nico pushed the computer aside and braced his elbows on the table. "Bryce, what do you think about getting more intel from your precinct? If the Death Rays are on their radar, they must have some idea about what they're involved in."

"I can try," Bryce agreed. "But keep in mind I was supposed to work today. I called off sick to help you out."

Nico winced. "Sorry about that."

"It's fine." Bryce shrugged off his concern. "Thankfully, tomorrow is a normal day off for me." The K9 cop turned thoughtful. "I'll make a few calls. See if I can come up with anything useful." Bryce rose and headed outside with Kirby at his side.

Zulu looked as if she wanted to go out too, but Nico gave her the hand signal to stay down. Then he glanced at Dawson. "Anything else you can think of that I should be doing? I feel like we're flying blind here."

"I know what you mean. But we know who the enemy is, even if we don't know exactly what they're up to." Dawson swept his gaze around the interior of the house. "If we were staying longer, I'd consider adding cameras, but trip wires should work well enough. Thankfully, we have enough manpower to keep two men here guarding the women. If you ask me, that's the most important thing."

"No argument there." If Nico could have kept Ava someplace behind steel walls and an electric fence, he would have. But the rental house would have to do. The men who would stay behind would die for her, as he would.

It gave him a twinge to leave Ava behind to investigate the warehouse, but he shoved the sentiment aside. He knew the layout of the warehouses better than the others.

And maybe he was secretly hoping to confront Simon too.

Mason returned with enough food to feed an army. As

they put things away, Ava came out to join them, looking adorably sleepy.

It was nearly impossible to stop himself from sweeping her close for a long kiss.

"I can help," she said, heading into the kitchen.

"You can follow the doc's orders by sitting and resting." Nico gently took her arm and ushered her toward a chair at the table. "Please."

She blew out a breath. "I'm not used to this."

"I know." He smiled. "But we have it covered."

"Looks like someone bought out the grocery store," she said with a laugh.

"Hey, seven men, two women, and three dogs need a lot of food," Mason joked.

"True that," Dawson added.

Nico was glad to have his teammates there for support. "We're planning a simple lunch in about thirty minutes or so. Just sit tight and we'll take care of bringing the food out."

"Thank you, Nico." Ava glanced around the room. "I notice a couple of guys are missing."

"They're sleeping. We'll all take a turn getting some rest," Nico explained.

"Makes sense. Is Callie still sleeping?"

"As far as I know." Nico gestured to the hallway. "Her door has been closed the whole time."

"I'm not surprised. This has been a lot for her to handle." Ava frowned as Bryce came over to sit beside her. "You're not planning to arrest her, are you?"

"Me? No, why?" Bryce appeared surprised by the allegation. "Has she broken the law?"

"We both have, yes. But only to survive." Ava sighed, then added, "You should know that Callie didn't get much sleep last night while she was held in the warehouse. She told me she feared Simon would come at any moment to kill her."

Bryce winced. "I'm sorry she had to go through that."

"Yeah, well, maybe go easy on her," Ava advised. "She knows Simon kidnapped her to get to me. She feels bad enough without fearing being arrested for past deeds."

"I'm not planning to arrest anyone except Simon and the Death Rays," Bryce said wearily. "Trust me, that will be more than enough paperwork to handle."

"Ava, Bryce has only been trying to help." Nico understood Callie's fears, but he felt they were unfounded. "Risking his own job to do it, I might add."

"I explained that to Callie," Ava said. "Give her some time, I'm sure she'll come around."

"She can have all the time she needs. My goal isn't to make her uncomfortable, but I can't change the fact that I'm a cop." Bryce rubbed the back of his neck, glancing down at his German shepherd. "She should know that once this is over and Simon is no longer a threat to either of you, she never has to see me or Kirby again."

Ava nodded, then slowly rose. "I'll check on her. Let her know lunch will be ready soon too."

Nico wanted to tell Ava to sit back down, Callie was an adult, she could come out of her room in her own time. Yet he managed to hold back. For one thing, it was clear Callie and Ava had been depending on each other over the past few months. And for another, he needed to have faith in Ava's ability to recognize any signs and symptoms of preeclampsia and to take action to mitigate them. He had to admit, Ava looked much better now that she'd taken a nap.

"I'm going to pull the food out now," Kaleb announced. "That way people can eat when they want."

"I'm hungry," Dawson said with a grin.

"You're always hungry," Mason muttered. "Must be all those abdominal surgeries you had."

Nico hung back as the guys joked around. His own stomach was in knots, but he'd eat to keep him focused. He frowned when Ava hurried down the hall from Callie's bedroom. He quickly went to join her.

"Easy, don't rush," he admonished.

Ava gripped his arm. "She's gone."

"Who, Callie?" Nico inwardly groaned. They so did not need this.

"Yes, Callie." Ava leaned against him. "It's my fault, Nico. Callie has been worried about what we're going to do when this is over. She has some wild idea that I don't need her anymore. I tried to reassure her that we'll stick together once this is over, but I must not have gotten through."

"It's not your fault, Ava, it's hers. She made the decision to leave." Although why the woman would do such a thing was beyond reason. Callie should have waited until they'd gotten the evidence they needed to put Simon and the other Death Rays behind bars.

"We need to find her," Ava said, "before Simon does."

"No." Nico wasn't about to go chasing after Callie again. Not when she'd chosen to leave. "We're not doing that."

"What's this about Callie?" Bryce asked, heading over to where they were talking.

"She's gone, Bryce." Ava sniffed and swiped at her eyes. "I'm worried about her."

"Stress isn't good for the baby." Nico was upset with Callie for adding to Ava's stress level. As if she didn't have enough to worry about already.

"Kirby and I will find her," Bryce said.

Nico eyed him warily. He hated to lose a helping hand,

but he could also understand why Bryce would want to find Callie. "Are you sure?"

"Kirby's an excellent tracking dog. I'll use clothing from her room to put him on the scent." Bryce hesitated, then said, "If you think you can spare me. I don't want to leave you guys high and dry. So far my contacts within the department haven't gotten back to me."

"We're good," Nico assured him. "If you think Kirby can find Callie, then go for it."

"Thanks." Bryce took Kirby into Callie's room.

Nico watched them go. Maybe Bryce and Kirby would be back in time, but there was no guarantee.

One thing the SEALs learned was to roll with the punches. The plan would be adjusted accordingly.

Tonight, they'd get what they needed to put Simon away once and for all.

---

NICO WAS angry with Callie for leaving the safe house. Ava could hardly blame him. But other than refusing to go searching for the missing woman, he simply gathered at the kitchen table with his teammates and altered their plan.

"Kaleb and I will take the warehouse alone," Nico said. "I want two men to stay here at the house to watch over Ava."

A few of the guys exchanged knowing glances, but no one argued. "That's fine," Mason finally said. "Two-man teams will work."

"We need a guy to accompany Dallas to the docks," Nico said.

"I'll go," Mason volunteered.

Ava swallowed hard at the thought of Nico volunteering to go back to Simon's warehouse to look inside the crates. She wished he'd have taken boat slip thirteen instead, but both places were likely dangerous.

And Nico was personally invested in bringing Simon down. The warehouse was probably the fastest way to do that.

But also more dangerous.

*No stress*, she reminded herself.

"The food is ready, let's say grace." Kaleb bowed his head and spoke out loud. "Lord, we thank You for this food we are about to eat. We ask for Your continued guidance as we continue to seek justice. Amen."

"Amen," the group answered simultaneously.

Ava was amazed that this group of strong military men weren't afraid to pray in public. Both Kaleb and Nico had taken the lead in prayer, but she knew any of the others would have stepped in if they hadn't.

Jaydon, too, if he were still alive.

Her gaze clung to Nico as he moved around the kitchen. She was about to join him when he caught her gaze and waved her back. "This plate is for you."

The sweet gesture nearly brought tears to her eyes. She blinked them back, wishing the hormones would cut her some slack already. Everything—happy thoughts, and sad ones, made her weepy these days, and she didn't like it.

"Thank you." She took the plate from Nico's hands. "That's way too much food, though."

"You're eating for two," he teased.

Yeah, she didn't need a reminder. The only time she could see her toes was when she propped her feet on a pillow.

Nico joined her a few minutes later. Dallas and Hudd came out of the bedroom and dug in to the simple fare too.

"Looks like we're just in time," Dallas drawled, his Texas accent stronger than usual. "Y'all didn't leave much for us."

Mason grinned. "You snooze, you lose."

That elicited a round of chuckles. Ava found herself surprisingly envious of the camaraderie they shared. They had a closeness that wasn't very common these days.

Which only made her think about Callie's leaving.

She knew Callie had suffered substance abuse issues in the past. Not in the months they'd spent together, but several years earlier. As upset as Callie had seemed about hearing the news of her pregnancy complications, Ava feared Callie might spiral down that dark path again.

But she hadn't mentioned her concerns to Bryce. Maybe she should have, but adding to the dislike between them hadn't seemed wise.

She leaned toward Nico. "Bryce will call or text you when he finds her, right?"

He nodded. "Yes. But keep in mind, searching for a single woman in a city the size of Los Angeles won't be easy. The dog will help track her to a certain extent, but the minute she hops on a subway or bus . . ." He shrugged.

"Yeah, that's what I'm afraid of," she confessed.

"Listen, Ava, I know you care about your friend. I do too. But you have your baby to worry about. And that means not stressing over things you can't change."

He was right, so she nodded. "I know."

He took her hand. "God will watch over Callie, Bryce, and Kirby. We need to have faith that this is all part of God's plan."

"I've never really believed in God's plan, but now?" She took a moment to absorb the teamwork and friendship between the men. "I do." She turned toward Nico. "I know

God sent you to find me when I needed you the most. So thank you, Nico. Thanks for being so stubborn and tenacious about tracking me down."

He grinned. "You're welcome. I'm glad my mule-headed tenacity worked out for a change."

She couldn't help but return his smile. "You're a good man, Nico."

His cheeks flushed, and he shifted uncomfortably. "Not that good," he muttered in a low voice.

She wasn't sure what that meant, but he turned his attention to the protective Doberman. Zulu was never far from his side. "What's wrong, you have to go outside?"

Zulu got up and took a few steps toward the door, then turned back to make sure he was coming. She hadn't noticed the dog trying to get his attention, but now it was clear the animal needed to go out. Ava had to smile at the way Nico carried on his one-sided conversations with the K9.

"Hudd and Dallas, you guys are on KP duty," Mason said. "Who wants to hit the rack next?"

"Think that should be you, old man," Kaleb said.

The rest of the guys snickered.

"I'll go, but a second man needs to get some shut-eye too. Kaleb, I see you recently volunteered. Good job. Oh, and since we have another bedroom now with Callie gone, a third guy can use that to sack out for a while too."

Kaleb groaned but nodded. "I'll take the spare room."

Dawson sighed. "Guess that leaves me to sleep with the boss."

More snickering as the guys playfully punched each other in the arm. She loved watching them interact, it made her feel closer to Jaydon in some way.

Seconds later, though, a dull throbbing started in her

left temple. Ava reached up to massage it away, doing her best to ignore the tingle of fear that rippled down her spine. What if her blood pressure decided to spike again?

No, that wasn't going to happen. She closed her eyes, tuned out the men around the table, and concentrated on taking slow, deep breaths.

*Stay calm*, she inwardly whispered. *No stress. All is well.*

The voices around her faded as she imagined looking out at the Pacific Ocean, catching a glimpse of a whale fin slapping the surface before disappearing beneath the surface. She loved seeing whales and tried to imagine she was floating in the water beside them without a care in the world.

"Ava? Are you okay?" Nico's voice was low and husky in her ear. Oddly, she wasn't startled by his presence, instinctively knowing he'd come to her.

"Working on it." She didn't want to worry him mere hours before he was taking on Simon and the Death Rays.

"Do you feel sick to your stomach?"

"No, just a small headache." She was so focused on her breathing that she wasn't prepared for Nico to abruptly lift her into his arms. Her eyes widened, and she instinctively grabbed onto him as he carried her into the bedroom, much the way he'd carried her away from Simon's warehouse earlier that morning. "I'm too heavy," she protested.

"Not even close," Nico responded. Using his elbow, he pushed the door open and carried her sideways into the room. There, he carefully set her down on the bed. She straightened her sundress, surprised he wasn't breathing heavy from the exertion of carrying her. She was weighed at the hospital and knew she wasn't a lightweight. "Bed rest means staying in bed from now on, understand?"

"That's not what the doc said," she protested. "He said I could walk to the bathroom and to the kitchen for meals." She moved over, making room for him to sit beside her. "And that's all I've done."

"No reason to walk into the kitchen, we'll bring the food to you." Nico frowned at her. "And I know you're scared about Callie, but Bryce and Kirby stand the best chance of finding her."

"I know, and I'm not worried about Callie as much as I'm worried about you going to Simon's warehouse." There, she said it. Her feelings for Nico wouldn't be a secret for much longer.

"Ah, Ava, I'll do everything possible to come back without a scratch." Nico stared at her for a long moment, then slowly gathered her into his arms and kissed her.

She clung to his broad shoulders, reveling in the strength of his strong arms. This time, the kiss wasn't rushed but long and sweet and heady.

So much so, she never wanted it to end.

# CHAPTER THIRTEEN

Nico lost himself in Ava's kiss, secretly acknowledging this was what he'd wanted from her for years. Since the first time Jaydon had brought him home to meet his family twelve years ago.

Beautiful, sweet Ava had been just twenty years old at the time and off-limits. He'd known and accepted that fact. A man didn't make a move on his best friend's sister. Especially one that was eight years younger.

Yet here he was kissing the daylights out of her now.

He forced himself to break off the kiss, gulping air to infuse his brain with oxygen. He'd poured everything into their embrace and needed to find some semblance of control. His mind wasn't firing on all synapses, that was for sure.

"I—uh," he floundered, trying to come up with something intelligent to say. "I probably shouldn't have kissed you since you're supposed to be resting." How was that for inane?

"I don't think the doctor meant I couldn't hug and kiss a man," she said dryly, a hint of sadness in her gaze. "Don't worry, I'm not going to stress over it. I understand you care about me as Jaydon's sister."

"You're more than Jaydon's sister to me," he said rather impulsively. "I care about you. And little Jaydon or Jayne too."

"I care about you, Nico." She sighed and tucked a stray curl behind her ear. "Which is why I need you to promise me you'll be careful tonight."

"I will." He didn't minimize her fear, she knew first-hand what Simon and the other Death Rays were capable of. "And I want you to know that even if something happens to me, the other guys will step in to help take care of you and the baby."

That made her frown. "I don't need them to take care of me. I can take care of myself and the baby."

He let that slide, knowing that it wouldn't matter if she wanted their help or not, she would get whatever she needed and more. "I've been in more danger than this, and God has always watched over me. I don't go into an op with fear. I go in determined to get the job done to the best of my ability."

"I trust in your knowledge and skills." She managed a smile, then added, "And I believe God is watching over all of you too."

He was touched by her renewed faith. "God is watching over all of us, including you, Ava."

She nodded but didn't say anything more. Nico forced himself to step back from the bed. "I'd like you to rest for a while. Will you do that for me?"

"I'll do that for you, me, and my baby." She rubbed her abdomen. "I'm sure we'll be fine."

He wished he was equally sure. There hadn't been much time to research preeclampsia, and while he knew

Ava would do her best to control her stress, the phenomenon didn't seem to be just related to stress.

What had the doctor said? One theory was that the woman's body was reacting negatively to the baby?

He hated to think about how Simon had forced himself on Ava. Considering what she'd been through, she was handling the pregnancy very well.

At some point, though, the reality of the situation might rear its ugly head. And if that happened? Nico planned to be there for her.

No matter what.

He left Ava to join the others.

"How is she?" Dallas asked with a concerned frown.

"She's fine. But we need to make sure she stays off her feet as much as possible." He raked his hand through his hair. "That includes taking her meals to her rather than having her join us out here."

"Not a problem," Hudd drawled. "She won't have to lift a finger."

"That's what I told her." Nico had known the team would rally around Ava. "Thanks, guys."

"No thanks needed," Dawson said. "We're here for Jaydon's sister and his niece or nephew."

"Let's get back to the plan for tonight." Nico took a seat at the table. "I know we should wait until three or four in the morning, but I'd like to get in and out earlier if possible."

"I was thinking about that." Hudd leaned forward. "Going to slip thirteen earlier might be smart if we want to catch them in the act of unloading product. We could do that first, then head to the warehouse."

Nico swept his gaze over the other SEALs. "Thoughts?"

Dallas shrugged. "It's one approach, but splitting up to

hit both places at the same time stretches their resources too."

"Yeah." Nico rubbed the back of his neck. "I can't lie, I'd feel better splitting up and hitting them both. We risk going to the pier and finding nothing when I know for sure there are crates in the warehouse."

"Unless they've moved them," Hudd pointed out.

"You mean to the main warehouse?" Nico blew out a breath. "That's possible. But there were so many crates in that warehouse I find it difficult to believe they'd have room to fit all their merchandise in there."

"Simon could find another spot to keep the stuff, but that might take time. And some of his guys will be hurting today." Dawson shrugged. "I know I gave a few of them pretty bad headaches."

Nico wished Mason and Kaleb were here to add their thoughts. Not that he begrudged them time to sleep, but he could have used the wisdom offered by their senior chief. He told himself to go with his gut. "I think we should split up and go to both target locations at the same time. If we find it necessary to adjust the plan, we let the other team know."

"Works for me." Dallas finished his meal and stood. "Come on, Hudd. Let's clean up the kitchen."

The rest of the day passed slowly. When it was Nico's turn to sleep, he found it difficult to deploy the tactics that had served him well during their military ops. Memories of kissing Ava intruded on his thoughts, distracting him.

Especially since she'd eagerly kissed him back. In a way he'd only dreamed about. He couldn't be sure, though, that she hadn't just kissed him out of loneliness. Or simply out of fear of losing him. After all, he was the only thing standing between her and Simon and his motorcycle gang, the Desert Death Rays.

One kiss, well, two kisses did not equate to declarations of love. To be fair, Ava was hardly in a position to fall in love, even if she was so inclined. Her focus should be on her baby. And staying healthy.

Something he'd do well to remember.

When dinnertime rolled around, Nico checked in on Ava just as she was getting out of bed.

"Where are you going?" He hurried over to her side. Zulu, his constant shadow, came with him.

"Bathroom first, then to the kitchen." Ava smiled. "I smell something great."

"Spaghetti seems to be Dallas's new favorite meal." Nico smiled wryly. "He's even making garlic bread. Go ahead and use the bathroom, then I'll carry you to the kitchen."

"No! I'm too heavy for you to carry me!" Ava flushed with embarrassment as she turned away. "I can walk just fine, see?"

Nico didn't answer, waiting patiently for her to finish up in the bathroom. When she emerged, he couldn't help but notice how beautiful she was. The way his chest tightened warned him he was treading on dangerous ground with her.

If he wasn't careful, she'd steal his heart.

As if she hadn't done so already.

"I'm not sure why I'm hungry, considering I've done nothing but lie around all day." She grimaced, carefully stepping around Zulu. "I'd prefer to be active."

"I know, but you'll do what's necessary anyway." Without giving her a chance to protest, he stepped forward and swept her into his arms. Zulu moved back as if trying to understand what was going on.

"Nico, I told you I'm too heavy."

"Okay, first of all, you're not too heavy at all, and it's insulting to me that you think I'm so weak I can't carry you. Secondly, you're on bed rest. So you either let me carry you into the kitchen or I bring you a tray in here." He paused in the doorway, staring down into her blue eyes. "Which is it, Ava? Kitchen or tray in your room?"

"Kitchen." She sounded annoyed, but he didn't care.

"Okay." Using his elbow, he pushed the door open. "Come, Zulu," he said. Thankfully, his K9 partner moved out of the way, giving him room. As he crossed the threshold, his left ankle twinged with pain, but he ignored it. The Achilles tendon that had been repaired still hurt on occasion. He knew the pain and discomfort was just something he'd have to learn to live with.

After setting Ava down in one of the kitchen chairs, he dropped beside her. Zulu would get her dinner once the humans were finished. The spaghetti dinner and garlic bread was already on the table. Kaleb took the lead role in saying grace.

Nico was surprised when Ava took his hand in hers beneath the edge of the table.

"Dear Lord, we are grateful for this wonderful meal You've provided for us," Kaleb said. "We ask You to continue blessing us as we seek justice for Ava, Callie, and the others who have been hurt by Simon and the Death Rays. Please also keep us, especially Ava and her baby, in Your loving care. Amen."

"Amen," Nico and Ava said at the same time. He gently squeezed Ava's hand. She appeared humbled to have been called out for a special blessing.

"Thanks for making dinner, Dallas." Ava smiled at the blond Texan. "It looks and smells amazing."

"Spaghetti is a staple in our house as it's Laney's favorite." At her confused glance, he added, "Laney is my daughter. The one I didn't know I had until she was eight years old."

"Oh, wow, that must have been difficult for you," Ava murmured.

"Not as hard as it was for Maggie to have been pregnant and alone while I was deployed overseas," Dallas admitted. "She married another man, but things didn't work out between them. Thankfully, she's forgiven me, and we're married now." The grin on Dallas's features was infectious. "I'm blessed that God brought me back into Maggie's and Laney's lives when they needed me the most."

"Amen to that," Dawson drawled.

Nico had mentioned Dallas's situation to Ava earlier, but it helped to hear it firsthand. He gave Dallas an imperceptible nod of appreciation for bringing it up. Hopefully, the news helped Ava understand there was no reason to feel uncomfortable about her situation.

When they were finished eating, Nico lifted Ava from the chair and carried her to the bedroom. Thankfully, she didn't bother arguing this time, likely figuring out it would be a waste of breath.

"Will you let me know when you're leaving?" Ava asked once she was situated in the bed, propped up against the pillows.

"Yes. We have some time yet before it gets dark." He tucked the blanket around her. "Can I get you anything?"

"No, I'm fine. Thanks, Nico."

"Anytime." He didn't want to leave, but they needed to

get ready. He'd need time to scope out another location to leave his SUV. "Come, Zulu."

The Doberman licked Ava's hand before turning to follow him out of the room. He took a few minutes to feed her. Kaleb did the same with Sierra.

Three hours later, they were preparing to leave. Nico and Kaleb had both decided to leave their respective K9s behind again because of the motion sensor cameras. Mason and Dallas left at the same time as they'd need to check out the marina in general before setting up a place to watch slip thirteen.

Once they were geared up, the four men double-checked their communication systems. One of the headsets was damaged, so Mason swapped it out for a different one.

"All set?" Nico glanced around the group. They all nodded in agreement. "Let's go."

The city of Los Angeles was never fully dark, not with all the lit buildings, car headlights, and streetlights around. After thirty minutes of driving around, Kaleb and Nico found a new location to leave their SUV.

They sat and waited for another hour before stealthily making their way toward the storage warehouse.

The trip itself seemed to take forever. There were two guys posted on each side of the warehouse, so he nodded to Kaleb indicating they should take the two men near the back door out first. Kaleb would stay and take care of anyone else while Nico went inside to look inside a crate.

Easier said than done.

Nico managed to sneak up on the Death Ray, hitting him on the back of his head with the butt of his Sig Sauer. The big biker crumpled wordlessly to the ground. At the same time, Kaleb took out his man too.

Nico didn't waste a second easing inside the warehouse.

He was prepared to find more guards, but surprisingly, the area appeared empty. He carefully approached the closest crate and used his MK 3 blade to pry it open.

Inside, he found what appeared to be home decor. The benign front didn't fool him. Digging deeper, he found what he'd expected.

Bricks of heroin.

He took photos with his phone, then quickly left as silently as he'd come in. Kaleb was waiting, and seconds later, they were inching away from the warehouse.

As they slowly went down to the ground and slithered away, he thought, *Mission accomplished.*

THE BIGGEST RISK of bed rest was dying of boredom.

Ava stared up at the ceiling of her bed. Having a one-sided conversation with Zulu had helped pass the time, but the Doberman was sleeping now, leaving Ava with nothing to focus on but her situation.

And the sizzling impact of Nico's kiss.

This time, she knew she couldn't blame her hormones. She'd enjoyed every second of being held by Nico. He was tall, dark, handsome, strong, and an honorable guy.

Yet in the back of her mind, she couldn't discount the possibility that he cared about her as a woman he felt responsible for. Not one he'd have chosen to be with if not for her being Jaydon's sister.

Not to mention ending up in danger from a group of outlaw bikers.

Would Nico have looked at her twice if she'd remained in San Diego working her boring job as a dental hygienist?

Highly doubtful. No, Nico had specifically come to save

her from Simon. And while she was grateful, she couldn't fool herself into thinking there was more between them than friendship.

Besides, Nico could have any woman he wanted. Why would he be interested in her? Especially when she was as big as a baby elephant.

She shifted in the bed, trying to ease the pressure on her back. The male doc who'd ordered her to be on bed rest must not realize how uncomfortable it was to be in one position for any length of time.

*No complaining*, she sternly reminded herself.

Ava dozed for a while but was startled awake when Zulu abruptly jumped up from the floor, growling low in her throat.

"Easy, girl," she soothed while pressing a hand to her own heart, willing it to slow down to a normal rhythm. "Nothing for you to worry about."

She heard a door open and close, followed shortly by the low rumble of male voices. Being away from the others was wearing on her, so she rose and walked to the doorway. Zulu followed, clearly anxious to join the others.

Ava moved slowly, mentally checking for signs or symptoms of her blood pressure spiking. Thankfully, she didn't experience any headache or nausea.

There were four men in the kitchen when she approached. Hudd jumped up when he saw her. "You're not supposed to be walking," he scolded in a gruff voice.

"I'm fine." She took the closest empty chair and sat. "Nico is being a bit overprotective, but the doctor said I could walk to the kitchen for food and to the bathroom." She looked at the four grim faces of the men. "What's wrong?"

There was a long pause as the four SEALs glanced at

each other, no doubt trying to figure out how much to tell her.

She suppressed a sigh. "I'll worry more if you keep me in the dark about the danger."

"We're safe here," Mason said quickly. "I didn't notice anyone following us back from the marina. But as we approached slip thirteen, we were too late. A sailboat was already leaving, and there was no sign of the panel van."

"I see." She understood their disappointment. "Hopefully, Kaleb and Nico found something helpful."

"I'm sure they did," Dallas assured her. "We haven't heard from them yet, but they won't call until they're far away from the motion cameras."

She'd almost forgotten about Simon's cameras. Was it possible for Simon to have changed the sensitivity so that the cameras would pick up even the slightest bit of movement? Hopefully not.

Swallowing against the knot of fear in her throat, she strove to remain calm. Worrying wouldn't change the outcome.

"If we don't hear from Kaleb and Nico within the next thirty minutes, Dallas and I will head over to investigate," Mason said as if sensing her feelings. "We won't let anything happen to either of them."

"I know." As she pushed up from her chair, all four men leaped to their feet.

"What do you need?" Hudd asked.

"Yes, please sit." Mason gently pushed her back down. "Are you hungry? Thirsty?"

"I'd like a glass of water, please." She'd never seen four men trip over themselves like this. It would have been comical if it wasn't so sweetly serious.

Hudd filled a tall glass with ice water and brought it

back to her. Up close, she noticed his one eye didn't track the way the other one did. She vaguely remembered Hudd showing up to Jaydon's funeral with a patch over one eye.

"Thank you." She sipped the water, feeling extremely self-conscious as Nico's teammates closely watched her. "Do you mind if I ask why you're waiting thirty minutes before heading out to check on Nico and Kaleb?"

There was a long silence as the four men exchanged bemused looks. She was growing frustrated with their efforts to speak around her.

"Come on, guys, I'm right here." Her voice came out sharper than she intended. "Don't just look at each other, talk to me."

"We're not trying to avoid talking to you, Ava. To be fair, you're right," Mason said. "There's no reason a couple of us couldn't head over to the warehouse sooner."

"I'd feel better if you did," she said frankly.

"That's fine." Mason nodded and rose to his feet. "Although I'm sure Nico and Kaleb would find a way to let us know if they were in trouble."

She was about to argue when Dallas reached up to his earpiece. "We hear you loud and clear, Nico. Go ahead and give us the update."

After a few moments of listening, Mason said, "Roger that. We'll wait here for you and Kaleb."

The ball of fear lodged in her throat dissipated. "They're okay?"

"Yes, they're in the SUV and heading back here," Dawson told her. "They're roughly twenty minutes out."

That was very good news. "What did they find?" She hoped Kaleb and Nico's trip wasn't a bust the way Dallas and Mason's was. Otherwise, she'd never be free of Simon's threats to implicate her in Banjo's death.

"Several kilos of heroin in one crate, hidden beneath a bunch of home decorations," Hudd said with a grim smile. "Nico took pictures of the one crate he'd opened. Those should be enough to get a warrant to search the place. And it should also be enough to arrest Simon and the other Death Rays."

"You think so?" She was afraid to hope it would be that simple. "They'd have to prove it's Simon's, though, right? And what about the video?"

"No sign of that yet. I don't think Simon can pretend the drugs aren't his, though, considering they were found in the warehouse adjacent to where Simon and the others are living." Hudd gently patted her on the back. "Don't worry, this will all work out. No cop is going to believe other bikers are dealing drugs without Simon's knowledge. And in my experience, it only takes one man to turn on the others."

"I'm sure you're right." She forced a smile. Deep down, it wasn't easy to let go of the fear she felt toward Simon. In her heart, she knew her baby's father would pose a threat to her and the baby for as long as he was alive.

*Trust in God.*

Nico's husky voice echoed in her ear. And now that she'd experienced Nico's and the other SEALs' faith for herself, she knew he was right.

Having faith in the Lord would get her through this.

It was wrong to wish for Simon's death. The pictures were a problem yet too. But nothing she could fix now.

She heard Dallas explaining how he and Mason had arrived at the marina too late, the sailboat already heading out to sea. She couldn't hear Nico's response. That probably didn't matter now that they knew the Death Rays were buying and selling drugs.

Zulu and Sierra both stood and began to growl. She

frowned, wondering if the dogs didn't get along for some reason or if something else had captured their attention.

After all, Zulu had heard Dallas and Mason returning well before she had.

"Do you hear that?" Hudd asked.

Mason shook his head. "No, but the dogs do. Tell me what I'm missing, Hudd."

Suddenly she heard it too. And she could tell the others had as well. It was the distinct sound of a motorcycle engine.

And not just one bike, several.

Maybe even the entire Desert Death Rays motorcycle gang.

## CHAPTER FOURTEEN

Nico heard the rumble of motorcycle engines when he and Kaleb were still two miles from the rental property. Lots of motorcycles, at least a dozen, maybe more. His gut tightened as he understood the implication.

Simon had found Ava.

He wasn't sure how as he hadn't even gotten back to the rental property himself yet. Maybe someone had followed Dallas and Mason from the marina? They would have noticed a motorcycle, but traffic in Los Angeles meant lots of cars and other vehicles on the road.

"Mason, do you hear the motorcycles?" Kaleb's voice was calm in his earpiece. Nico tried to stay focused on driving, but his attention was diverted toward Ava and the rest of his SEAL teammates.

"Roger that. We're putting Ava in the main bathroom, the one that doesn't have any outside walls."

"Thanks. We're going to ditch the SUV and come in the rest of the way on foot," Kaleb said as Nico found a spot to pull off the road. The motorcycle engines grew louder, fueling him to duck down in his seat. He reached over to grab Kaleb's arm to pull him down too.

Bright headlights flashed by a few seconds later. He tried to count the lights, but they were close together. It didn't really matter as there were far more bikes than he had men.

One Navy SEAL was worth five guys, but he feared they'd still be woefully outnumbered. Not that it mattered. The entire team would take on the Death Rays, no matter how many odds were stacked against them.

It was like their last op all over again. Only this battle would be fought in an urban setting rather than in the desert of Afghanistan.

"Call 911 and get the cops there," Kaleb said to Mason as he slid out of the passenger door of the SUV.

Nico quickly got out of the car, too, and ran around to join Kaleb. He put his hand to his earpiece. "I'll call Bryce. He needs to know the Death Rays are converging on the safe house."

"Roger that," Mason said. "We'll be ready."

*Ready for war*, Nico thought grimly, but he didn't say it. He turned toward Kaleb. "We need to run. How will your knee hold up?"

"Probably about as well as your ankle." Kaleb flashed a grim smile. "It won't hold us back."

"Let's go." Taking the lead, Nico cut through the city streets taking a shortcut to return to the rental house. The roaring motorcycle engines were meant to be intimidating, and he silently prayed the police would get there very soon.

Before a barrage of gunfire broke out. From both the Death Rays and his teammates.

Four men against at least two dozen motorcycle thugs. He pushed the thought away, ignoring the pain in his ankle as he ran. If he and Kaleb could reach the house before the Death Rays had surrounded it, they'd have an advantage.

He desperately wanted to know Ava was safe.

After five minutes, he abruptly stopped and crouched at the corner of a neighboring property. Kaleb dropped down beside him. The houses were too close together to see much detail, but the motorcycle engines were loudly proclaiming their presence.

"Okay, let's go in through the back," Nico said. There was no need to whisper thanks to the Death Rays' motorcycles rumbling loudly enough to wake the dead. He touched his radio and told Mason the same thing so they'd expect them. Then he added, "If we stumble across any Death Rays, we take them down."

Kaleb nodded, and they both began making their way toward the rear of the house. Again, there was no reason for stealth, but it didn't take long to see two motorcycle riders standing in front of them, their gazes fixated straight ahead on the rental property. Each man held a gun in his hand, and they seemed to be waiting for the go signal to start shooting.

Nico gestured to Kaleb, indicating he'd take the one in front of him, leaving the second for Kaleb. For once, Nico was grateful for the noisy bikes as the two men never heard them coming.

It was tempting to simply kill them outright, but he settled for striking the guy sharply on the back of his head, sending him pitching forward to his knees. When he moved, Nico hit him a second time. Kaleb's biker ended up the same way, and they quickly dragged the unconscious men backward.

After reaching the side of the house, he approached the back corner cautiously. Yep, two more bikers were stationed back there too. Obviously, the bikes out front were mostly for show as an intimidation tactic.

The Death Rays already had the house surrounded.

He gestured for Kaleb. Taking these two out wouldn't be easy from this angle, so Nico made a circle motion with his finger, and Kaleb nodded in understanding.

They moved back to where they'd left the two unconscious men and continued circling the back of the neighboring house. From that position, they could better sneak up on the bikers.

Thankfully, the engines continued, so he and Kaleb were able to take those two men out as well. Once they'd dispatched those bikers, Nico hesitated, debating if they should take out the other two on the next side of the house or simply get inside before the gunfire erupted.

The decision was taken out of his hands when he heard the roar of several weapons being deployed at the same time. Bullets pummeled the sides of the house, shattering windows. He barged in through the back door, staying low and away from the line of fire.

"North and east sides of the building have been cleared for now, tangos on the south and west," Nico spoke into his radio, hoping he could be heard over the gunfire. "Two likely stationed on the west side, too many to count out front."

"Roger that," Mason called, his tone calm. Nico soon realized each of the SEALs had moved so they were near the windows on the west and south sides of the house. Every cell in his body wanted to find Ava, but he took up a position near the front window.

"Bryce is on his way and so are the cops," Dallas said in his ear.

"Roger," Nico responded, fearing that Bryce and the

police would be too late. The gunfire didn't cease, making it nearly impossible to get a shot off. Nico realized he and Kaleb had done better while staying outside, so he ran through the house to the back door.

"Nico? What's your twenty?"

"Heading outside to get rid of the tangos on the west," Nico said without stopping.

Seconds later, Kaleb joined him. "Same plan as before," he whispered.

Nico nodded. Ignoring the gunfire wasn't easy. He was getting the impression that the gunfire out front was a distraction and that one of the four men he and Kaleb had neutralized was tasked with going inside to find Ava.

The sooner they took out the other two men, the easier it would be to hold them off long enough for the cops to get there.

Although he couldn't figure out what was taking them so long. First Mason had called, and surely now others had called in the repeated gunfire.

He and Kaleb eased up behind the two men, only this time they must have been heard as the man in front of him abruptly turned with gun in hand.

Nico instinctively fired two shots. The biker stumbled and fell without getting a shot off himself. But he noticed the bedroom window was broken and surmised the guy was about to breach the house.

He belatedly realized Kaleb had shot his biker too. Seeing the man's gun still in his hand, he understood why. This situation was quickly spiraling out of control and made him concerned one or more of the four men they'd left unconscious would wake up and join the gunfight.

Seeing the window was that of Ava's room, Nico sent up a prayer of thanks that they were able to prevent these guys from getting inside. It was clear the bikers out front were firing nonstop as a distraction so the others could infiltrate the building.

He gestured for Kaleb to follow as he ran around the corner to head back inside. Six bikers were down, two dead, but there were still too many to count out front.

And from the brief glances he'd gotten of the six men he and Kaleb had dispatched, none were Simon.

"Kaleb, cover the back door."

His teammate nodded.

The gunfire abruptly stopped. In the nanosecond of silence, the wail of police sirens could be heard, but the noise was quickly hidden behind more gunfire, this time coming from within the house.

Mason, Dallas, Hudd, and Dawson were making their presence known.

The bikers roared away, which made him wonder about the four men he and Kaleb had rendered unconscious. He glanced over. "We need to see if the four guys are still outside. If they are, we need to bring them in."

"Got it," Kaleb agreed. Before either of them could move, though, the return gunfire from their teammates abruptly ceased.

Nico knew that was because the bikers had scattered like rats. "I'm checking on Ava, you take the others out to get the bikers."

Without waiting for Kaleb to acknowledge his request, he spun and headed to the bathroom. He found Sierra standing guard outside the door and assumed Zulu would be inside with Ava.

"Easy girl," he said softly, reaching beyond the K9 to open the door. "Everything is okay now."

The door was locked. "Who's there?" Ava called.

"Nico." He was tempted to simply kick the door in but waited for Ava to unlock and open it.

"You're alive," she whispered, reaching out to him.

He swept her close, closing his eyes in gratitude that she wasn't harmed. The way the Death Rays had peppered the house with gunfire, he'd worried a bullet had punctured through one of the interior walls. "So are you," he whispered back.

She lifted her head and kissed him. Their embrace was all too brief, though, as the police sirens grew impossibly loud. Ava stepped back and rubbed a hand over her belly. "Did you see Simon out there?"

"No." He frowned when he noticed a small hole in the wall above the toilet. One of the bullets had found a way inside after all. He took both of her hands in his. "Ava, are you sure you're not hit?"

"Yes. But that bullet was awfully close. Zulu is fine too," she hastily added as he dropped his gaze to his partner. "I have no doubt she would have bitten anyone who dared to come inside."

"She's a good protector," Nico agreed. The bullet hole still bothered him, and he swept a gaze over the floor until he found the bullet fragment. He reluctantly released Ava to pick it up. "I'm glad neither one of you were hit by this."

Ava blew out a heavy sigh. "I was so worried about you."

"Same goes." He took her arm and led her out of the room. "Tell me the truth, Ava. How are you feeling? Do you have a headache? Feel sick to your stomach?"

She hesitated, then said, "A slight headache, but that could be because of the gunfire not my blood pressure."

Nico felt certain her headache was a result of her blood pressure rising, but he didn't point it out. Instead, he bent to lift her into his arms and carried her into the kitchen. After setting her on a kitchen chair, he checked the back door. Kaleb was coming inside with a biker slung over his shoulders.

"Here's the first one." Kaleb set the suspect down on the floor.

Mason came in next. "Here's a second."

Ava's eyes widened in shock when she saw the unconscious bikers. Nico rummaged in a drawer until he found a length of rope. He tied both men together as Hudd and Dallas brought the last two men inside.

One of them was coming to, so Nico gestured to a kitchen chair. "Put him there. I'm sure the cops will want to talk to him."

"Roger that," Hudd said with a grunt. Nico quickly bound him to the chair while Dallas set his biker down beside the others.

"What happened?" The biker blinked in confusion, then looked horrified when he saw he was surrounded by the SEALs. "Who are you?"

"We're the men you tried to kill." Nico pulled out a chair, moving it so that he was facing the biker. "Where is Simon?"

"Uh—" The guy glanced nervously around the room, blanching when he saw the other three men tied together on the floor. "I don't know."

"Police! Come out with your hands up!" The shout came from out front where the bikers had been stationed just a few minutes ago.

Nico glanced over at Dallas who nodded. "I'll go talk to them, cop to cop."

"Good luck," Dawson drawled, slapping his swim buddy on the shoulder as he walked by.

"Where's Bryce?" Nico frowned. "I thought he'd be here to help take the pressure off."

"He said he would be here." Mason shrugged. "I didn't ask how far away he was, though."

Nico heard Dallas shout, "Don't shoot! I'm coming out unarmed!"

As if fighting off the Death Rays wasn't bad enough, now they'd have to prove their innocence to the local police. Nico turned his attention back to their hostage. "Did Simon send you to kidnap Ava?"

The biker darted a glance at Ava, then quickly turned away. "I want a lawyer."

Nico leaned closer, pinning the guy with a lethal stare. "Don't mistake me for a cop. Or these other men either. You're not under arrest, and I can easily kill you before the police get inside. These men will validate my story of self-defense. You have thirty seconds to tell me who sent you."

The biker glanced once more over at his three biker buddies. He swallowed hard, then whispered, "Simon. He wants the preggo."

Preggo? Nico barely managed to hold back from slugging the guy in the face. He slowly rose and stepped away before he could give in to the temptation.

Looking out through the shattered window, he could see Dallas trying to smooth things over with the cops.

All of this and they still hadn't gotten to Simon.

Nico could only hope and pray the pictures he'd taken of several kilos of heroin would be enough to nail him once and for all.

AVA LACED her trembling fingers together, hiding them from Nico's eagle eye. If he knew how close she was to falling apart, he'd rush her to the closest hospital.

A trip she fully expected to take sooner than later. Taking deep breaths hadn't eased her headache, at least not yet.

Gunfire pelting the house was probably not what the doctor had in mind when he'd told her to rest and relax.

She really, really didn't want to have her baby early.

"The police are coming in," Dallas announced.

Ava glanced at the biker Nico had tied to the chair. He avoided her gaze, staring at the floor instead. She recognized him as being part of Simon's Death Rays, but she didn't know his name.

Or the names of the other three men who were tied together.

She was secretly glad Nico had managed to tie up four Death Rays. Oh, she knew there were roughly forty bikers in Simon's group, but it seemed likely that these four would end up turning on their leader to save themselves.

One of them had already broken down to admit the truth.

She noticed Nico and the other SEALs holster their weapons, making sure their hands were out where the police could see them. A stream of officers came in, moving around the house.

Bryce was with them, and he nodded at her as if glad she was okay.

"This is Ava Rampart," Bryce said, introducing her to one of the cops. Based on the stripes on the guy's sleeve, she assumed he was in charge. "Ava, this is Sergeant Lowell. Ava was kidnapped earlier this morning from a local hospital by the Death Rays on orders from their leader,

Simon Normandy. She was taken to their warehouse and held in a locked room."

"Ma'am," the cop said with a nod. "Is that true?"

"Yes." She felt herself flush with embarrassment but forced herself to add, "I escaped Simon before he knew I was pregnant with his child. He was determined to get me back but didn't care that I was in the hospital for medical treatment."

"I see." Sergeant Lowell turned back to Bryce. "Go on."

"I worked with these former Navy SEALs to infiltrate the Death Rays warehouse to rescue Ava and another woman named Callie from the gang," Bryce said.

"Callie?" Sergeant Lowell interrupted. "Where is she?"

Bryce frowned. "She left on her own. I've been trying to find her, but so far I haven't been able to."

Sergeant Lowell frowned. "This is some story."

"It's all true, sir," Dallas said, stepping forward. "I mentioned I'm a cop with the Fredericksburg Police Department in Texas. This motorcycle gang is bad news. See that bruise on Ava's cheek? That's Simon's handiwork."

She wanted to hide but tipped her chin so the bruise was more noticeable. "These men saved me and my baby."

"I have proof the Death Rays are buying and selling drugs." Nico stepped forward, holding out his phone. "Kaleb and I sneaked into their warehouse again just an hour ago. I opened one of the crates and found this."

Sergeant Lowell whistled. "Heroin."

"Yes, sir." Nico nodded. "By the time Kaleb and I returned here, the Death Rays had the house surrounded. Kaleb and I took out these four men, and we were forced to shoot two others. They're on the west side of the property. They both pulled guns on us first, so we fired in self-defense."

Lowell sighed heavily. "There are two dead men out front as well."

"Yes, sir," Mason agreed. He stepped up to join the circle of men. "Dallas and I were watching the front. We were under heavy fire, as you can see by the multiple bullet holes in the siding and the shattered windows. We returned fire, striking two men."

The sergeant raked his gaze over the group of former SEALs, taking in their bullet-resistant vests and their holstered weapons. Ava had the impression he was considering taking them all into custody to sort out the details later.

"You heard the motorcycles," Bryce said, breaking the silence. "There had to be at least a dozen or more."

"And this guy"—Nico nudged the biker tied to the chair —"already admitted he and his pals were sent here by Simon to kidnap Ava, again."

"Okay, okay, I believe you." Lowell sighed, then pointed his index finger at Bryce. "I want statements from everyone involved, understand? No one leaves until I say it's okay."

"Yes, sir," Bryce responded. "That won't be a problem."

"Sergeant, will you please take these four men into custody?" Nico asked. "I believe once the other three come to, they'll be happy to cooperate."

"We want a lawyer," the guy in the chair muttered.

"Of course you do," Lowell muttered harshly. "That's fine with me. You don't have to say a word. The bullet holes in the house say plenty and provide more than enough evidence to hold you and your biker friends. Once we're finished processing the scene, I doubt there's a judge on the bench who would be willing to grant bail."

The biker sitting across from her swallowed hard and

looked away. Ava sincerely hoped he was coming up with a way to throw Simon under the bus to save himself.

A dozen police officers swarmed the place, moving inside and outside the property. She noticed Nico took Lowell into the bathroom where she'd been hiding with Zulu during the event, pointing out the bullet hole that had gone through the exterior and interior walls, nearly striking her.

"What I want to know is why this Simon wants her so badly?" Lowell asked with a frown. "Why take this risk, losing a total of eight men just for one woman?"

Ava froze, her heart thudding painfully against her chest. This was it. This was when the truth would come out.

A wave of nausea hit hard. She struggled to control the urge to throw up, knowing she was on the verge of getting arrested for killing Banjo.

"If you ask me, he wants the baby," Nico said. "I think he was going to hold Ava hostage until she gave birth, then take the baby from her."

"No way, that makes no sense at all," Lowell scoffed. "What would a biker do with a baby? I can't imagine any one of them taking care of an infant."

"Maybe he'd planned on keeping Ava long enough to care for the baby," Nico admitted. "He could still want an heir. Someone to take over the gang."

"That's a long way off," Lowell muttered. "And doesn't seem like the Death Rays' style. Especially since they're dealing drugs."

Clearly, Lowell wasn't buying Nico's theories. She tried to take a deep breath to bring her blood pressure down, but it was no use. The pounding in her temple intensified. She knew her preeclampsia had returned in full force.

Maybe this was God's way of telling her she needed to take responsibility for what she'd done.

"Simon wants me, not the baby," she managed.

"Ava, you don't know that." Nico rushed to her side, his dark gaze warning her not to say too much. "Simon is an evil narcissist. He probably thinks he'll be able to groom the baby to be like him."

"That's not the whole truth," she said, wincing as the pounding in her head grew even worse. She put her hand up to her head, striving to remain calm.

No stress, please, no stress.

"Ava? Are you okay?" Nico's tone changed to concern.

"Not really. I—" She abruptly clamped her hand over her mouth.

Nico instantly grabbed the kitchen garbage can in the nick of time. She threw up into it and then began to cry.

"She needs to go to the hospital," Nico shouted. "Now!"

"What's wrong?" Lowell asked.

"She has a condition called preeclampsia. High blood pressure causing headaches and nausea." Nico put a hand on her shoulder. "Stay calm, I'll get you to the closest hospital, okay?"

She nodded. The cops and SEALs jumped into action, one of them calling an ambulance, but she didn't move. Tears slipped down her cheeks.

She'd failed to keep her baby safe. If her symptoms were as bad as she feared, her baby would be born prematurely. And could even die.

*Please, Lord, protect my child!*

# CHAPTER FIFTEEN

"Where is that ambulance?" Nico scowled at his watch for the third time in as many minutes. "It should be here by now."

"You want me to run back to get the SUV?" Kaleb asked.

He hesitated, then turned toward Lowell. "I need one of your officers to drive us, red lights and sirens the entire way."

"Hold on, I don't like the idea of you leaving with her," Lowell protested. "You shot a man."

"In self-defense," he agreed, "which I owned up to. You don't seem to understand the seriousness of Ava's condition. She could lose her baby if we don't get her to a hospital right away. I'm going with her, end of discussion."

"The rest of us will stay as long as you need," Mason added. "We understand you have a crime scene to process."

"This is just one crime scene, but the warehouse is another." Hudd pinned Lowell with a narrow look. "You need to obtain a search warrant for Simon's warehouse to find the drugs."

"I'm getting sick of you guys telling me how to run the show," Lowell snapped. "You're not cops."

"No, but we do what's necessary to get the job done," Mason said.

Nico turned toward the officer closest to him. He was about to strong-arm the guy into driving them when he heard the ambulance approaching.

*It's about time*, he thought wearily.

And really, it was for the best. The paramedics would take good care of Ava, updating the hospital on her condition along the way. They'd know how to treat her blood pressure and how to treat any seizure she might have.

He prayed that wouldn't happen. The doc had diagnosed her with mild preeclampsia, but he likely hadn't expected that she'd be huddled in a bathroom with Zulu while bullets relentlessly pelted the house around her.

About as far from stress-free as you could get.

Nico was about to lift Ava into his arms, then stopped when the paramedics ran in wheeling a gurney. Ava looked pale and shaky as they approached.

"Thanks for coming." She managed a smile despite the tears that had dampened her cheeks. Watching her cry had been like a sucker punch to the gut.

"What's going on?" The taller male paramedic had a name tag identifying him as Marvin. "Are you having contractions?"

"No, my blood pressure is spiking." As Ava explained her symptoms and the diagnosis of preeclampsia, both paramedics looked grim. The female, named Lucy, proceeded to check her vital signs, starting with her blood pressure.

"How bad is it?" Ava asked.

"It's high at one eighty-four over ninety-eight." Lucy glanced at Marvin. "We'd better get her on the gurney."

Nico stepped back to give them room to maneuver. Once Ava was strapped onto the gurney, he moved alongside her with Zulu trailing behind as they headed outside.

"Hold on there." Marvin held up his hand. "Sorry, man, but you and the dog can't ride with us."

"Why not? Zulu won't hurt you."

"Not enough room back there," Marvin said firmly. "You can follow us to the hospital and meet up with your wife in the emergency department."

Nico didn't bother to correct him about his and Ava's relationship. As the pair of paramedics slid Ava into the back of the ambulance, he frantically glanced around. There wasn't enough time for him to get back to the spot where he and Kaleb had left the SUV.

Bryce came up beside him. "Come on, I'll drive you."

"Thanks." Nico gratefully followed Bryce and Kirby to his K9 vehicle. "I'm sorry you didn't find Callie."

"Yeah, me too." Bryce slid in behind the wheel and quickly fell in behind the ambulance. "I'm sure she can take care of herself, but I can't help worrying the Death Rays will find her."

"Maybe not now that we've taken out eight of their men while preventing them from kidnapping Ava." Nico wished they'd have gotten to Simon too. Was the guy out front the whole time, hanging back from a secure location? Or was he a big coward who had stayed back at the warehouse while his minions carried out his orders?

*Probably the latter*, he thought sourly.

"I'm sure Sergeant Lowell will follow up on the Death Rays' drug trade," Bryce said reassuringly. "He's a good cop."

"Yeah, but not until he's finished processing the crime scene, right?" It was during times like this that he missed working with the SEAL teams. Their hands hadn't been tied up in yards of red tape. They'd gone in, executed their mission as ordered, and then sat through a debriefing afterward.

When that was finished, they moved on to the next op.

He tried not to think about how Simon could right now be orchestrating a plan to move all drug product from the current warehouse to another secret location. It's what he'd do in his shoes.

If not for Ava's tenuous medical condition, he'd ask Bryce to take a detour past the warehouse to check on things. But he told himself to leave the criminal aspect of the Death Rays in the hands of the local police.

Especially since he and Kaleb weren't entirely in the clear after the way they'd shot two Death Rays members.

Nico shoved that thought aside. He needed to stay focused on the task at hand, which meant supporting Ava through this crisis.

Praying her baby wouldn't suffer the consequences.

The ambulance vanished from his line of sight, but Bryce seemed to know where he was going. Roughly ten minutes later, Bryce pulled his vehicle into a hospital parking lot near the emergency department. Nico recognized it as the same one he'd taken Ava to after rescuing her from Simon's warehouse. No doubt, it was the closest medical facility.

He hoped the medical staff would decide to admit her for observation this time. It bothered him to think her lack of insurance had caused the doc to send her home rather than keep her as an inpatient.

"Do you want me to stay with you?" Bryce asked.

"No, thanks." Nico pushed open his door to climb out.

He let Zulu out too. "You should head back. Make sure Lowell treats the SEALs fairly."

"Okay, if you need something, call." Bryce gave him a nod. "And don't worry about your buddies. They'll be fine. Lowell isn't going to come down hard on any of you. Not after the way those Death Rays shot up the house."

"I hope you're right about that." He shut the door, then took Zulu over to a grassy area so she could take care of business. When that was finished, he headed inside the emergency department.

The place was super busy, so he had to wait in line before he could talk to the receptionist. "I'd like to see Ava Rampart, please."

"Have a seat, I'll let the staff know." The woman appeared frazzled as she put a note in the computer. "Next?"

Swallowing a sigh, he headed over to find an empty seat in the waiting room. Zulu stretched out at his feet, drawing several gazes from other patients and families.

He ignored their stares, wishing he'd have pushed harder to ride with Ava in the ambulance. Being separated from her like this was agonizing.

He wanted to be there for her. Not just now but always.

Because he loved her.

The realization hit hard, but it also gave him a sense of peace. He was tired of fighting his feelings. He loved her now and always. The only problem was that he had no clue how she felt about him.

He was determined to find out. Not now but when the time was right.

The adrenaline rush faded, leaving a keen exhaustion in its wake. He stood and went over to the coffee machine. Finding a few crumpled bills, he fed them into the machine and then gratefully took the coffee back to his seat.

Based on the thrum of activity in the waiting room, Nico knew he was in for a long wait.

---

AVA COULD TELL by the way the nurse had rushed off to call for an OB doc that they were concerned about her and the baby.

She allowed her eyelids to close, wishing Nico was there. In the short time they'd spent together, she'd grown dependent on his unwavering support.

Reminding herself that it was far better to remain independent, she shifted to a more comfortable position. She'd find another dental hygienist position and move on with her life. Nico would stop in and check on her, but imagining some sort of fairy-tale ending was a path to heartbreak.

Besides, Nico deserved better than a woman carrying another man's child.

A tall man wearing scrubs and a face mask entered the room. At first she assumed he was the OB doc, but then his gaze locked on hers. An icy chill coalesced around her.

Simon!

She reached for the call button but missed. Simon lunged toward her, his large hands closing around her neck, squeezing tightly. "This is for Banjo," he whispered harshly.

No! She would not let him kill her and their baby!

She rattled the side rail, kicking him with her feet. His hands gripped tighter, and she could feel her lungs burning for air.

"Get off her! Attack, Zulu! Attack!" Nico's voice held a note of desperation as he rushed forward.

Zulu leaped up and sank her teeth into Simon's arm. He cried out in pain and released her. Stumbling back, Simon tried to hit Zulu with his free hand.

Nico grabbed onto him, flinging him like a rag doll across the room with impressive strength. Simon hit the wall with a hard thud, then slowly sank down.

The door to her hospital room swung open, and several medical staff members came into the room along with a security guard.

"Put your hands where I can see them," the security guard shouted.

"Not me, him. He tried to strangle Ava," Nico said, pointing at Simon. "You can see how he's dressed as a hospital staff member."

"Nico is right. That man tried to kill me." Ava pushed the words through her bruised throat. Even though Simon had only attacked her for a few minutes, she could feel her throat start to swell from the intense pressure.

Just like the last time he'd tried to choke her to death.

The security guard must have believed her because he used his radio to call the police, then stepped toward Simon. "You need to come with me."

Simon abruptly sprang up, slamming into the security guard and knocking him backward. Then he bull-rushed the staff around her bed. The two nurses and doc stumbled back, leaving a clear path to the door.

No! He was getting away!

"Get him," Nico shouted, and Zulu once again sprang into action. She leaped toward Simon, clamping onto the edge of his scrub top with her teeth. It was enough to stop Simon momentarily. Nico didn't hesitate to leap forward, jumping on top of him and taking him to the floor.

"You're not escaping this time," Nico said, pressing

Simon down against the hard linoleum floor. "Cuffs! I need handcuffs!"

The security guard managed to get to his feet. He joined Nico, helping to cuff Simon. When they had Simon secured, Nico turned to his dog.

"Are you okay, girl?" Ava watched as he ran his hands over the Doberman, making sure the animal hadn't been injured. "Are you okay?"

"That dog bit me!" Simon screamed. He looked like a cartoon figure with his mask half on and half off his face. "I'm pressing charges, you hear me?"

Nico ignored him, lowering his head to Zulu. "Good girl, Zulu. You're a very good girl."

"She saved me." Ava reached up to touch her sore throat. "You both did."

"What's going on here?" Another man in scrubs entered the room, looking around at the stunned expressions on the faces of the staff. He gestured to Simon. "Who is that? Does he have a hospital ID badge?"

"No, sir, he does not." Nico stepped forward, taking control of the situation. "His name is Simon Normandy, and he's the leader of the Desert Death Rays motorcycle gang. He's been trying to kill Ava for the past few days and almost managed to do that here. Oh, and he also deals drugs out of his warehouse in town. If you call Sergeant Lowell with the LAPD, he'll fill you in."

"Yeah, okay, but who are you?" the doc asked. "You're not supposed to have a gun in here."

"Nico Ramirez and my K9 partner, Zulu." Nico pulled his weapon and handed it butt first to the security guard. "Sorry about that, but I've been keeping Ava safe, so it's been a necessity. I'm an honorably and medically discharged Navy SEAL."

"Impressive, but medically discharged?" The doc raked his gaze over Nico. "You look fit to me."

"Ruptured Achilles tendon on my last op. Can't run the way I used to." Nico gestured to her. "Ava is my fiancée. I respectfully request your team take Simon out of here so she can get the care and treatment she needs. He tried to strangle her and likely injured her windpipe."

"I'm fine, Nico." She inwardly winced at the hoarseness of her voice. "It's not as bad as the last time he did this."

"Last time?" one of the nurses echoed in horror.

"I'd rather the doctors take a look at your throat anyway." He came over to take her hand. "And how are you feeling otherwise?"

Before she could respond, two uniformed LAPD officers came into the room. Nico looked extremely frustrated for a moment. Then he quickly kissed her. She had to swallow the insane urge to giggle, something she hadn't done in months since being on the run, as Nico turned and painstakingly went through the entire sequence of events yet again.

"Any reason why he's so determined to get to Ms. Rampart?" one officer asked.

Before Simon could respond, Ava quickly said, "Yes, because I killed his best friend, Banjo, months ago while escaping Simon's motorcycle gang." She boldly admitted her crime, feeling a massive wave of relief for having the secret out in the open.

"Ava, don't," Nico protested, but she waved him off.

"I regret killing Banjo, I didn't intend to do such a thing. But I don't regret escaping Simon that night." She swallowed hard, then added, "As you can see from his actions today, I knew it was only a matter of time before he succeeded in killing me."

"Again, talk to Sergeant Lowell," Nico said firmly. "The Death Rays just shot up the safe house we were using to shelter Ava. We managed to take out eight of his biker buddies, four are dead, the other four are in police custody. Oh, and I have proof he's dealing heroin."

That news seemed to deflate what was left of Simon's bravado. "I don't know anything about a shootout or heroin," he protested weakly.

"How did you find us here?" Nico asked. "You were hiding like a coward watching the entire thing go down."

"No, I don't know anything about it . . ." Simon's voice trailed off.

"Yeah, that's what they all say," one of the cops drawled. "Let's go. The other charges will be added later, I'm sure. For now, you're under arrest for attempted murder."

Ava watched with relief as the officers dragged Simon from her room. It was over. Thanks to Nico and Zulu, she and her baby were safe.

Mostly safe. She still might end up in jail at some point. But not yet. She rubbed a spot on her belly where the baby was kicking. Maybe they didn't want her in jail if she was destined to deliver her baby nearly eight weeks early.

"I'm Dr. Robertson," the tall man introduced himself. "I'm here to examine you and your baby." He glanced at Nico. "Obviously, your fiancé is welcome to stay if that's what you'd like."

"Yes." Ava knew she should correct him, but since Nico started the charade, she went along with it. "I'd like Nico to stay."

Dr. Robertson did a very thorough exam, including peering down her throat to assess the damage Simon had inflicted. When he seemed satisfied she was doing okay, he asked the nurse to check her blood pressure again. It was better but not back to normal.

"We'll need you to stay for observation," Robertson said. "While reading your medical record, it appears you left AMA, against medical advice, yesterday."

"No, that's not true. I was foolish enough to go down to the cafeteria, and I was kidnapped by one of Simon's biker friends." She gripped Nico's hand. "I would never leave against medical advice. I want my baby to be healthy. I've been trying to follow doctor's orders by staying on bed rest. Obviously, I haven't been able to avoid stress until now."

"I see." Robertson nodded thoughtfully. "I'm sorry to hear you've been in danger. Don't worry, we'll take good care of you. As soon as a room becomes available, we'll take you upstairs to the OB unit."

"Thanks, doc," Nico said.

As soon as Dr. Robertson and Shelia the nurse left, Ava let out a heavy sigh. "I can't believe it's finally over."

"I can't believe you told the cops about killing Banjo," Nico chided. "You didn't have to say anything, Ava."

"Yes, I did." She turned to look at him. "It was time to take responsibility for my actions. Maybe Simon would have still come after me if I hadn't killed Banjo, we'll never know for sure. When I think about how much danger I put you and your friends in . . ." She blinked back tears. "I never wanted anyone to get hurt. I should have just come clean a long time ago."

"Hey, don't cry." Nico's dark eyes held a note of panic as he gently reached up and wiped away her tears. "You're safe, and the rest of the SEAL team is too. That's all that matters, Ava."

"Oh, Nico. I'm not sure what I did to deserve you," she whispered.

"I'm the one who is blessed to have you, Ava." He bent his head and kissed their joined hands. "I love you. Not just because you're Jaydon's sister but because I've always had a crush on you."

A crush? Really? Her heart swelled with hope, even as she didn't quite believe him. "Come on, Nico, you never acted interested in me."

"Only because Jaydon told me you were off-limits." Nico's smile held a note of sadness. "I miss your brother, but he's not here, Ava. And I'm tired of hiding my true feelings for you. I understand if you don't feel the same way. You've been through a lot these past few months, and I don't want to rush you into something you're not ready for."

She searched his gaze, wishing she could read his true feelings. Was he just saying this to make her feel better? Or was he being honest?

It was impossible for her to know.

"I care about you, Nico. But I'm pretty sure you don't want to raise another man's baby."

"Wrong answer, Ava." His tone was light, but his intense gaze was not. "I love you. I've never said those three words to another woman. And I wouldn't say them now if they weren't true."

Oh, how she longed to believe him. Still, she hesitated. This was hardly the time and place to make life-altering decisions.

"Have faith, Ava," he said in a low husky voice. "Have faith in God and faith in me. I love you, and I will love our child too."

There was no mistaking the love shining from his eyes. She had to blink back more hormone-laden tears. "I do have faith in God and in you, Nico. I've always been attracted to you, but I assumed you only thought of me like an annoying younger sister." She pulled him toward her. "I've fallen in love with you too."

"Ah, Ava." He lowered his head and kissed her. It wasn't a quick embrace either, he took his time exploring her mouth, making her dizzy with desire.

"Hey now, I'm not sure that's what the doctor meant when he ordered strict bed rest," Shelia teased as she entered the room. "Kissing is okay, but nothing more strenuous, understand?"

Nico lifted his head, but his gaze lingered on her mouth. "I love you so much," he whispered, before straightening. Then he flashed a grin at the nurse. "Yes, ma'am."

Ava flushed with embarrassment, knowing Nico was playing up his role as her fiancé, pretending to be the baby's father.

"Should I give you a few minutes before checking your blood pressure?" Shelia arched a brow. "I wouldn't want it to be falsely high because of a potent kiss."

"Um, maybe." She felt her cheeks heat even worse than before.

"What's the status on her room?" Nico asked, changing the subject.

"Still working on that," Shelia admitted. "We've been incredibly busy lately. There are rooms, but they need to be cleaned."

"I'll clean one," Nico offered. Ava thought he was joking, but his gaze was serious. "Give me the supplies and I can get it done in no time."

"That's a nice offer, but they're working on them." Shelia eyed him curiously. "You really would clean a room for your fiancée?"

"Yes. Of course."

"He's a keeper," Shelia said to Ava.

She managed a smile. "Yes, he is the best man I know."

Shelia took her blood pressure, then checked her other vital signs too. "Your blood pressure is almost within normal limits."

"Great news," Ava murmured.

After Shelia left, Nico pulled his chair closer to hers. "Ava, I know this might be rushing things, but I want you to consider becoming my fiancée for real. Will you please marry me?"

Her heart swelled with love. If it were up to her, she'd marry him right away, but he didn't know what their lives would be like once Jayne was born. "Maybe you should wait to see what it's like being a full-time parent. This may turn out to be more than you bargained for."

"Ava, this is our child. Yours and mine. We'll raise him or her together, and like every other pair of first parents in the world, we'll figure it out as we go along." He took her hands in his. "I love you. I want to marry you. If you need time, that's fine. But don't use the baby as an excuse."

"Jayne is not an excuse," she protested. "I'm just worried you'll be overwhelmed with everything."

"If I can handle twenty years as a Navy SEAL, I'm pretty sure I can handle a few dirty diapers." His wide grin faded. "Ava, I'm looking forward to our time together as a family. We can wait until after the baby is born, if that's what you'd prefer, but I want to marry you. As soon as you're ready."

"Yes, Nico." There was no point in fighting her feelings. She loved Nico more than she thought possible. "I would be honored to marry you. As soon as we're able."

"Good. That's great." He looked relieved, as if he'd really doubted she'd agree to become his wife. "Hey, maybe the hospital chaplain can marry us?"

She had to laugh. "Maybe, but if not, there's no rush. I'm not running away again, Nico. I'm here to stay."

"Me too." He bent and kissed her again. "I'll always be there for you, Ava. Now and for the rest of our lives."

"And I'll be there for you too." Marriage was a two-way street. They'd both have to work at it to succeed.

But there wasn't a single doubt in her mind that they would.

# EPILOGUE

*Two weeks later . . .*

"Sit down if you feel faint," the anesthesiologist said sternly. "Do not mess with or fall into my equipment."

"I won't. SEALs don't faint."

"Famous last words," the anesthesiologist muttered. "I've seen plenty of big, strong men hit the floor."

"Not me." Nico was determined to make good on his promise. He stood at the head of the operating room table, dressed in scrubs, a paper gown, a mask over his face, and a bonnet over his hair. Ava was lying before him, her belly exposed as the staff washed it with a cleaning solution to prepare for an urgent C-section.

Not an emergency, Robertson had said. But urgent. So here it was, first thing in the morning, and they were ready to go.

In the two weeks since Simon's arrest, Nico and Kaleb had been cleared of shooting the two Death Rays bikers, and Simon was facing several charges—attempted murder, kidnapping, assault and battery along with drug trafficking. The Feds had gotten involved in the drug trafficking since

Simon was bringing them in with help from a Mexican cartel. The pictures and video of Ava killing Banjo had been found in the warehouse, but after the prosecutor had heard from Ava personally, he'd declined to charge her with any wrongdoing. Nico was relieved about that. From what he'd heard from Sergeant Lowell, Simon would be locked up for a long time. The rest of his SEAL teammates had returned to their families, although they'd insisted they'd be back for the wedding.

Today, he'd been forced to leave Zulu in a kennel. The hospital leadership had flatly refused to allow a dog, even a service animal, in the operating room.

He figured Zulu would understand. He and his K9 had been spending a lot of time at the hospital. Even while being inpatient and on medication, Ava's blood pressure would occasionally spike, sometimes to dangerous levels. After the most recent episode, Dr. Robertson had finally decided it was time to deliver Ava's baby. He'd done an ultrasound and confirmed the baby was about five pounds. And since inducing labor would only increase Ava's blood pressure, they'd decided to perform a Cesarean section.

Ava tightened her grip on his hand. "I'm worried I'm going to feel the scalpel," she whispered. "I can feel them tugging on my belly."

"Doc?" Nico called. "Are you sure the epidural is working?"

"Do you feel this?" Robertson used the sharp point of a needle to tap her skin.

"No," Ava admitted.

"Good, you'll be fine. The epidural takes care of the sharp pain, but you'll feel us take the baby out. I promise it won't hurt."

"Are you sure?" She didn't look convinced.

Nico bent his head close to hers. "Let's pray, Ava. Lord, give Ava the strength she needs to undergo this procedure. Please provide these doctors and nurses with incredible skill as they deliver our baby. And keep our precious child safe in Your care. Amen."

"Amen," Ava echoed.

Nico was so engrossed in their prayer that he missed the initial incision. Seeing the blood, he swallowed hard. It was far more difficult to watch the woman you loved being cut open than he'd anticipated.

*No fainting!*

There were other staff members standing near a high table covered with bright overhead lights radiating warmth on the blanket below. Robertson had explained that when the baby was born, they'd put the infant in the warmer to do a quick assessment. If the baby was stable, they'd bring the child to Ava for skin-to-skin contact.

"Spreader," Robertson called. A moment later, he asked, "Ready?"

"Yes, doctor," the nurse near the warmer responded.

In a blur of motion, the baby was delivered through the opening in Ava's stomach. It happened so fast Nico barely had time to react. Thankfully, he didn't feel the least bit faint. The miracle of birth was something to behold, even though this wasn't the way Ava had wanted it.

God had other plans.

"You have a healthy baby girl," Robertson announced. Seconds later, she began to cry. "With a nice set of lungs too."

"Really?" Ava looked dazed. "She's healthy?"

"Her crying is a good indication that she's doing well," Robertson said reassuringly.

Nico watched as the team wrapped the baby in a blanket, carried her to the warmer, and quickly examined her. Jayne cried the entire time, which Nico took as a good sign.

Robertson had assured them that a baby's lungs developed quicker while under stress. It was the same thing the other OB doc had told him, and based on Jayne's crying, it seemed they were right.

"Here you go, Mom and Dad," the nurse said, bringing Jayne over to them. They drew Ava's gown down a bit so the baby could rest against her chest. Nico reached over to place his hand over the baby's back. Jayne's crying quieted as she rested against her mother.

"Oh, Nico. She's beautiful, isn't she?" Ava asked, tears of happiness rolling down her cheeks. "Jaydon would be so proud."

"He would, and yes, Ava. You are both very beautiful." Nico's voice was thick with emotion as he gazed down at the amazing gift God had blessed him with.

His family.

I HOPE you enjoyed Nico and Ava's story in *Sealed with Valor*. This was going to be the last book in my Called to Protect series; however, I've added a Christmas novella just for fun. Are you interested in reading Bryce and Callie's story in *Sealed with a Christmas Promise*? Click here!

# DEAR READER

I hope you've enjoyed my Called to Protect series! I've had a lot of fun writing these books, and *Sealed with Valor* was no exception. I was happy to bring all the Navy SEALs back together again for a very special mission.

When I was pregnant with my first child, I suffered from preeclampsia. My daughter Nicole was born six weeks early via C-section because I was so sick. You'd never know it now; she's a tall, smart, and beautiful young woman. I used my experiences during those weeks of my pregnancy when writing about what Ava was going through, and I hope some of that reality came through.

I've also decided to write a Christmas novella featuring Bryce and Callie. *Sealed with a Christmas Promise* will be available on October 17, 2022. That will formally wrap up this series.

I adore hearing from my readers! I can be found through my website at https://www.laurascottbooks.com, via Facebook at https://www.facebook.com/LauraScott Books, Instagram at https://www.instagram.com/laurascott books/, and Twitter https://twitter.com/laurascottbooks.

Also, take a moment to sign up for my monthly newsletter to learn about my new book releases! All subscribers receive a free novella not available for purchase on any platform.

Until next time,

Laura Scott

PS: If you're interested in a sneak peek of *Sealed with a Christmas Promise*, I've included the first chapter here.

# SEALED WITH A CHRISTMAS PROMISE

## Chapter One

Callie's smile froze when she caught a glimpse of a familiar face as a man entered the diner accompanied by a large, imposing dog. What in the world was Bryce Flynn doing here? Their gazes locked, his intense green gaze seeming to look right through her. It wasn't easy to shake off the impact of Bryce's presence as she continued performing her duties, taking the coffeepot around to refill her customers' mugs.

Her mind whirled as she made small talk. She couldn't imagine why Bryce and his K9, a beautiful German shepherd named Kirby, had shown up here at Darla's Diner. They didn't see cops dropping in for breakfast on a regular basis, this area wasn't part of the usual cop beat. Then again, Bryce wasn't dressed in his cop uniform. Did that mean he was off duty?

She hated to admit how handsome he looked in his quilted vest and long-sleeved, checkered flannel shirt accompanied by a pair of worn jeans. She much preferred his casual look to the uniform he normally wore. December in Los Angeles could be cold, especially this early. Seven thirty in the morning to be exact. She frowned. It seemed awfully early for him to be up and about on his day off.

Yeah, the more she thought about it, the more she knew there was no way Bryce's being there was an accident. No, somehow, he'd tracked her down.

The better question was why he'd bothered? She self-consciously tugged at her ill-fitting, puke-green polyester uniform, wishing she was wearing something nicer. Ridiculous thought because she had nothing to prove to Bryce Flynn. She didn't much like him. It had been roughly two months since she last saw him. After he'd rescued her from the Desert Death Rays motorcycle gang, stashing her and her friend Ava in a safe house for protection. Oh, he'd been nice enough, until she'd realized he was a cop. That made him off-limits.

Logically, she knew there were good cops and bad ones.

She seemed to only find the bad ones.

She'd felt guilty about leaving the safe house so soon after he'd rescued her, but she had known it was for the best. However, she'd been completely stunned to see the news brief the following morning about a shootout involving the Death Rays. Her gaze had been glued to the television mounted high in a corner of the subway station as she'd recognized the house that had been riddled with bullets as the same place she'd sneaked away from mere hours earlier.

At the time, she'd worried about Ava's safety. They'd lost their cheap, disposable phones, so she couldn't check up on her friend and former coworker. For several days, she'd lived in fear her friend was dead and her baby, too, until she'd caught a brief clip of Ava and Nico leaving the hospital together. The press had jumped on the story of the pregnant woman who'd escaped the Death Rays with the help of several former Navy SEALs and had given birth to a baby girl.

Jayne. Callie's heart had twisted with regret when she'd heard the news. She'd wanted to be there with Ava when she gave birth. She and Ava had joked about whether she was having a girl or a boy. Callie kept calling her stomach Jaydon, while Ava had insisted the baby was Jayne. Apparently, Ava had been right.

She missed her friend, more than she could have imagined. Once, she and Ava had planned to relocate to Mexico after her baby was born.

But Ava had found Nico Ramirez, or rather, Nico had found Ava. Instantly, she'd known the two would end up together. And she was happy for her friend. Truly happy. Ava deserved to be loved by a man like Nico.

A happily ever after she'd never know.

"Hi, Callie."

She jerked, sloshing coffee from the pot when Bryce called her name. He'd taken a seat in an empty booth along the row of windows facing the street. She drew in a deep breath and forced a smile. A customer was a customer, and a tip was a tip. She needed every dollar she could earn during her shift.

"Hello, Bryce. Coffee?"

"Yes, please."

She filled his cup, avoiding his gaze. "Welcome to Darla's Diner. I'll be back once you've had a chance to review the menu." Their plastic menus were on each table in the form of a place mat. Yeah, this place was hardly high-class, but the food was decent. She'd needed money, and Darla, the owner, hadn't asked many questions. Callie had been grateful for the opportunity, especially since she was working two jobs. Her day job was here at the diner, but she also worked in another restaurant, too, on Friday and Saturday nights. A restaurant called The Flame.

There, the owner made her wear a low-cut, skintight uniform, which she hadn't liked. But the tips were great, so she'd gritted her teeth and put up with the groping customers.

Yet she was still behind on her rent. No surprise since she hadn't found anyone to help share a place with. At least, no one she trusted. One of her fellow servers at The Flame had offered to move in with her, but the way Stacy had fawned over her customers, even going out with them after work, made Callie suspicious she was doing more than serving them drinks.

Nope. Callie wasn't on board with that kind of thing.

"Any chance you have time for a break?" Bryce cradled his mug in his hands. "I'd like to talk."

The tiny hairs on the back of her neck lifted in warning. "We don't have anything to discuss. And no, I don't get breaks." That wasn't entirely true, once the morning rush had passed, she was able to grab a few minutes, but talking to a cop wasn't something she wanted to do while on break.

Or off break.

Or ever.

She quickly turned away, grateful one of the orders had come up. After delivering the two breakfast platters laden with food to her customers, she reluctantly returned to Bryce's table.

Pulling out her notebook, she stood with her pen poised over the pad. "Are you ready to order?"

"Veggie omelet, please."

She lifted her brow but wrote down the order. Most people who came to Darla's Diner preferred food laden in grease. Fried eggs, bacon, sausage, potatoes, etc. Was Bryce some sort of health nut? Maybe. His muscular physique was an example of how much he worked out. His strength was intimidating, but she did her best to ignore that. She might not trust Bryce, but he didn't come across as an abusive man either. Beneath the table, Kirby shifted into a more comfortable position. "Got it."

"Callie, wait." He caught her arm as she moved away. "What time do you get off? I really need to talk to you. It's about Otto."

The name of the Death Rays biker she'd briefly spent some time with caused ice to congeal in her veins. "What about him?"

There was a brief pause before Bryce responded. "He's dead."

She blinked in surprise, then shrugged, feeling her muscles relax in relief. Otto being gone was one less problem for her to worry about. "Don't expect me to cry any tears over that news."

"Have you seen him lately?"

A flash of anger hit hard. The idiot motorcycle gang member gets himself killed and she's a suspect? And wasn't that the story of her life. "No." She yanked out of his grasp and was about to walk away when she slipped on a spot of coffee she'd dropped on the floor. She lost her balance and fell forward just as there was a loud crack followed by the glass window of the café shattering into zillions of pieces.

"Callie!" Bryce lunged from the booth seat to cover her with his body. She hit the linoleum floor hard beneath his weight. She heard Kirby barking, and it took her a minute to understand what had just happened.

Someone had tried to kill her.

No, not her. Maybe Bryce. He was a cop and had no doubt made many enemies along the way. And hadn't Bryce just told her Otto was dead? If anyone had asked, she'd have named him as the most likely guy to come after her with a gun.

"I'm a cop. Everyone stay down and remain calm," Bryce ordered in a commanding tone. She felt his weight shift as he pulled his cell phone from his pocket. "This is off-duty K9 Officer Bryce Flynn and Kirby. Shots fired at Darla's Diner in west Los Angeles. Requesting backup and a bus."

Callie tried to move out from beneath Bryce's heavy weight, but it was impossible. The guy was built like an offensive lineman for the Rams. Kirby crawled forward on his belly from beneath the table to be near them. She couldn't deny having a soft spot for dogs. In her opinion, Kirby was Bryce's only redeeming quality. "Let me up."

"Not until the police are on scene." His tone was calm, then he raised his voice to ask, "Anyone hurt? Please remain calm, an ambulance will be here shortly."

A chorus of negative replies echoed around the café, although from her spot beneath Bryce, she couldn't see anyone. "If someone is unconscious or dead, they can't respond," she whispered.

"I know," Bryce agreed, his voice low and husky near her ear. It reminded her of the night he'd rescued her from the Death Rays warehouse where she'd been chained to the bed after being kidnapped from a restaurant in San Bernardino. He'd risked his life back in September to free her from the motorcycle gang. It was ironic that he was here with her again now. "My goal is to keep them calm until the police arrive."

That was understandable, and to be honest, he was doing a good job. Maybe because he'd announced himself as a cop, there was less panic and screaming.

*Or maybe they'd gotten too accustomed to violent crime in the city*, she thought wearily.

There was no more gunfire, leaving her to believe the shooter was long gone. She was about to tell Bryce that, too, but held her tongue upon hearing the approaching sound of police sirens.

"Stay down with Kirby, okay?" Bryce lifted himself off her, and she turned to look at Kirby. The large German shepherd was almost nose to nose with her, and he surprised her by licking her cheek.

She couldn't help but smile. How the dog remembered her, she had no idea. Well, other than she knew this particular K9 was incredibly smart and well trained. She reached over to pet his sleek fur. The dog helped calm her racing heart.

Cops swarmed the place, and soon she was helped to her feet by a uniformed officer. She instinctively moved away from him to check on her coworkers and other customers.

Incredibly, no one was seriously hurt. Some had sustained cuts from flying glass and bruises from hitting the floor, but nothing worse.

Which brought the entire incident right back to her. To the fact that the shooter had only one target in mind when he aimed and fired his weapon.

To kill her.

Her knees went weak. She sank down into the closest empty seat. Just the thought of starting over in a new place made her want to scream in frustration. Running from one place to another was wearing her down. At twenty-eight, she felt twice her age.

Who wanted to kill her, and why? Obviously, someone

who wasn't Otto. Without answers to those two questions, she'd have little choice but to move on.

Again.

And alone.

---

BRYCE SWALLOWED A WAVE OF FRUSTRATION. The cops were doing a good job in processing the scene, but he wanted to wrap things up here very quickly so he could take Callie someplace safe.

If she hadn't slipped, she'd likely be dead right now. Just like Otto.

He sent up a silent prayer of thanks to God for watching over them. Especially Callie. He'd known she was working at the diner now for the past few days but hadn't wanted to scare her off. The last time they were together, she'd run away, leaving the safe house rather than sticking around him and his SEAL buddies. He'd tried to find her, but it had taken far longer than he liked to admit to track her here.

His goal was to approach her one day after work, just to make sure she was doing okay. But then he'd learned Otto Redmond had been killed at close range by a shot to the heart with a small caliber pistol.

His mind had gone straight to a woman as a suspect. Any other perp who'd been that close would have shot him in the head. But the heart? That seemed to indicate a woman had done him in.

Otto hadn't been a nice guy, far from it. Bryce had no doubt the guy had made dozens of enemies while hanging with the Desert Death Rays, and he had likely killed people too. But murder was murder, which meant Otto was now a victim. While Bryce was off the clock today, his goal had been to talk to Callie before anyone from the homicide squad uncovered her previous relationship with the dead man.

That she had a possible motive for killing him.

"What makes you believe Ms. Burgess was the intended target?" Sergeant Grossman pinned him with a keen gaze.

"Because she was the only one standing in the line of fire." He didn't want to go into Callie's past, especially not now. He rested his hand on Kirby's head, keeping the K9 close. "If she hadn't slipped and fell as the gunfire rang out, she'd be dead."

"Hmm." Sergeant Grossman raked his gaze over the area for a moment, then asked, "And how do you know Ms. Burgess?"

"I hardly know her, we met briefly a few months ago." That was true. Bryce didn't want to lie, but he didn't want to implicate Callie more than necessary. Keeping his responses brief and truthful was the best he could do. Especially knowing Callie was in danger from some madman with a gun.

"I've taken her statement." Grossman frowned. "She claims she has no enemies, no one who would want to kill her. Furthermore, she seems to think you were the target."

He swallowed a groan. No surprise Callie was trying to deflect the attention away from her and onto him. It was annoying how much she didn't like him. He'd never hurt her, just the opposite. He'd helped her escape the Death Rays. He shrugged, keeping his tone even. "Anything is possible, but if I was the target, the shooter was off by a mile."

"Yeah, okay. We'll continue to work the scene. We found the shell casing, it's for a nine-millimeter handgun."

Nine-millimeter handguns were a dime a dozen in this city. It seemed like every single perp he came across had one. That alone wouldn't help, but maybe if they could find the slug? He thought back to the scene at the diner, those seconds when Callie had slipped as the glass shattered beneath the force of the bullet. "I believe the shooter was standing relatively close. If he was far away, it wouldn't be as easy to see inside the diner in broad daylight."

"Good point," Grossman agreed.

"You might want to check the counter for a bullet fragment." Bryce was glad there hadn't been a customer seated in the spot along the counter where Callie had been.

"Yep, got the crime scene techs working on that."

"Good." He tried to think of anything else that may help with the investigation. It was tempting to mention Otto, but the guy was dead. Yet he had no proof Otto's murder and this attempt to shoot Callie were related.

Unless, of course, the pair had made someone mad? Maybe the same shooter had done both deeds?

If that was the case, he'd need to come clean with the sergeant. But he needed more time to talk to Callie first. No easy task since she not only didn't like him, she also didn't trust him.

Despite the way he'd saved her life.

Not that he was looking for an award or anything. Saving people and keeping them protected was his job. But he wasn't sure he deserved her dislike and distrust either.

Whatever. He glanced down at Kirby. They were a good team. Kirby loved him no matter what. And Kirby had been his constant companion since he'd lost his wife three years ago.

Grossman waved his hand. "You and Kirby can leave, I know it's your day off."

"Thanks." He'd been keeping an eye on Callie and saw her huddled with Darla the cook and another server, the one who worked behind the counter. Both women were in their midfifties, which was probably why Callie's job had been to take care of waiting tables. Less walking around for the other two. He led Kirby over to where the three of them were sitting just outside the damaged building.

"Callie? Are you ready to go?"

For a moment, her eyes narrowed, but she must have reconsidered a negative response because she nodded. "Yes, but can you help Darla and Pat understand how long the café will be a crime scene? This is their livelihood."

"The scene will be cleared in an hour or two." He turned toward Darla. "You need to call your insurance company about getting the glass window replaced. Once that's done, you can reopen."

"I have. They're sending someone out this afternoon." Darla glanced around, seemingly depressed. "I'll still lose at least two days of business, maybe more because we're closed on the Christmas holiday."

"I'm sorry." He truly felt bad for her and those who worked in the café, but there wasn't anything he could do to change the timeline. He could, however, pay for his meal. He pulled out his wallet and gave Darla more than double what his bill would have cost. "I'm sorry for what you're going through."

"Thank you so much." Darla pocketed the money. Callie shot him a surprised look, then for the first time since he'd met her, she smiled.

"Yes, thanks." She stood. "I better go. Both of you take care, okay?"

"You too. I'll call you when we've been cleared to

reopen for business," Darla said. "I'll even pay you to help clean the place up if you'd like."

A flash of regret darkened Callie's eyes, but she smiled again and responded, "Sounds great." As she turned away, Bryce knew she was lying. She wasn't planning to come back to work at Darla's Diner.

She was planning to do what Callie did best.

Run.

Made in the USA
Columbia, SC
12 April 2024

34303786R00134